Angel Revenge
Blue Phantom Book Three

Vijaya Schartz

Print ISBN's
Amazon print 9780228632269
Ingram Spark 9780228632276
Barnes & Noble 9780228632283
BWL Print 9780228632290

Dedication

To the young at heart, everywhere, who still
believe good can triumph over evil

Table of Contents

Chapter One

Valka never tired of flying on Sultan... not a bird or a horse, not even a dragon, but a majestic tiger, the finest beast in all the realms. The morning breeze carried the dewy scent of grass and flapped the many flaxen braids flowing out of her top knot.

She patted the cat's muscular neck. "Good boy, Sultan."

The tiger leaned his head against her hand and gave a contented snort, baring sharp fangs.

"Sultan like cuddle." The beast's mind voice held pure adoration.

As they rounded a green hill, Valka heard explosions in the distance to the left. Her bare thighs clenched down as she leaned over for a panoramic view of the land below.

An after-battlefield, like thousands she'd seen before. Bright flares, fire, and thick smoke still obscured the grassy land. As the explosions relented, brainless robotic soldiers scoured the expanse, exterminating the hopeless and taking the salvageable survivors as prisoners... or slaves. Black floating craft, like ominous roaches, combed the ground, beaming up fresh bodies for spare parts and bio-materials.

The exact image of her vision. Valka had to hurry before the victors killed or stole her prize, though she wasn't worried about being seen in invisibility mode. Besides, no one had ever been able to catch her, even less hold her.

She pointed with her spear. "Sultan, bank left. That battlefield is where we land."

"*Sultan see.*" The magnificent tiger tossed his big head and with a slow flap of his wings, angled down in a wide swoop.

It seemed this green planet was being forced into submission by an army of black automatons. In Valka's experience, a local lord hungry for land wouldn't use sophisticated robots, or collect bio-materials.

Only a rising galactic empire could afford such an expense. Most likely, this fancy automated army belonged to the Priory and its creepy Abbotts, to expand their influence. They'd been attacking many planets lately.

But these details didn't concern Valka. Since her own world had been shattered millennia ago, she had seen many regimes rise and fall. She no longer cared about who fought whom, or for what reason. She just carried on her sacred purpose.

Holy visions showed her the brave, the pure of heart dying in battle, and Valka chose to save whomever she deemed worthy. It was her fate, determined long ago. Today, she had come for one soul... She could feel him close, heartbeat weakening, his lifeblood seeping into the muddy grass... dying way too young... not quite yet a man.

"Sultan, land at the foot of these trees by the river." Valka must retrieve her prize, before the robots finished him off, or the body harvesters snatched him.

"*Sultan see.*" The tiger veered and landed on a green patch, in a graceful arabesque, then retracted his magnificent wings.

Valka made herself visible again, unwilling to scare her target. She vaulted off the feline, and Sultan proceeded to lick his paws.

Adjusting the many weapons weighing her belt, Valka ran toward a young man lying in the grass. She enjoyed the heavy gravity, the thump of her boots on soggy ground. So close to the surface, the breeze carried the ripe and musty smell of death.

When she reached the young man, he was staring at the sky. The expanding blood stain on his green uniform jacket indicated a blade had pierced his chest. He didn't have long to live.

"Am I dead?" He blinked then focused on her. "Are you an angel?"

"By Odin's beard, no! Angels wear white. They have blue eyes and wings." Valka was tired of being mistaken for one. "My armor is blue, and my eyes are peridot green… my mother was Zephyrian."

"The Zephyrians are all dead. They were mind-readers, not warriors." He coughed some blood. "They didn't fly on tigers either."

A mine exploded close by, sending dirt and leaves in the breeze. The smell of burned flesh reached Valka's nostrils. "We have to hurry."

The wounded man lifted his head with great effort and narrowed his dark eyes on her. "What are you?"

"You ask too many questions." Valka never revealed her true nature. "You are too young to die. Be happy I decided to save your life today… but there is one condition."

"What?" His voice weakened. He grimaced.

She steeled herself against his pain. "Come with me, and you can live forever… but you will have to battle for a worthy cause."

He frowned.

Didn't she make herself clear? "Confusing, I know. There is always another great battle. Choose to fight in the next one, or die and be harvested for your bio fluids." Valka sighed. She'd missed her own final battle long ago. "Please, be smart. Don't squander your second chance at life. I need a decision this second."

The young man managed a weak smile. "Whatever you say, lady." He let his head rest on the grass. "I want to live."

"Good choice." Valka applied her hand on his chest. Light surged from it. "This will stabilize you." Then, she whistled three notes of a nightingale song.

"*Sultan ready.*" The majestic tiger loped to her side in a slow, deliberate stride.

The young man's eyes rounded at the sight of the beast getting so close.

Valka chuckled. "Don't worry. Sultan doesn't kill... unless I tell him to."

The tiger grunted in agreement.

"Let's hurry. The harvesters are getting closer." She lifted the young man in her arms. He didn't weigh much for a warrior. She flung him across Sultan's back. "Just hang on."

"Yes, Ma'am." He struggled to breathe. "What... worthy... battle?"

"You talk too much. Save your breath." Valka didn't want to chat, or know his name, or hear his thanks. In her line of work, friends were a burden, a hindrance... and they could get you killed.

Blaster shots sizzled close to her ears. She ducked and some bushes behind her caught fire. "Helshades!"

She stared in the direction of the shots. A brief movement, the flash of sunlight on metal. She drew her blaster, aimed and fired. A sizzle, the muffled thump of a hard body falling, then a burnt metal smell filled the air. "Got him."

She patted Sultan's flank. "The soldiers spotted us. Time to disappear."

The tiger's tail twitched. *"Go where?"*

"Byzantium!" She vaulted on Sultan in front of her prize.

The magnificent beast deployed his wings and took flight. *"Sultan like Byzantium."*

"I know you do, Sweetheart." Valka rejoiced at a good day's work. This young warrior, valiant and fully trained, would fetch a high price. Her current employers had deep pockets. That's how she could afford a marvel like Sultan.

Closing her eyes, Valka focused her mind. She felt the familiar tingle as she dematerialized the three of them.

* * *

General Konrad Lagarde flapped his wings and alighted on the marble floor as he materialized in the Temple of the Formless One, on the Byzantium Space Station. He retracted his wings, slicked back his short black hair, and straightened his white uniform. Then he scanned the place with all his senses.

Sweet fragrances of incense lingered in the air and soft harmonies filled his ears with calming energy. The sound emanated from the large Blue Crystal floating near the top of the crystalline dome. The luminous boulder reflected on all the polished surfaces and gave the entire temple a bluish radiance. The crystal sword at his side glowed brighter.

Small groups of angelic friars in white robes spoke in hushed tones, commiserating or congratulating each other. But some spoke loudly, smiled and even laughed... in a sacred place? How disrespectful!

Konrad shuddered. This entire station lacked discipline... another loosey-goosey enclave, where civilian angels had free will and played fast and loose with the rules... like on the *Blue Phantom*, which Konrad intended to whip into shape.

A friar in white hooded robes, arms crossed inside wide sleeves, shuffled toward him, smiled, then bowed. As he straightened, the friar pushed back his white hood. He didn't look entirely human, despite the smooth face and blue eyes... probably a mixed breed. Angels came in all shapes and sizes.

The friar bowed exposing the blue striations and folds on his scalp. "General, we have a new contingent for you to take to Azura."

"Good. Prepare to transport them to the *Blue Phantom*." At least, on Azura, these new recruits would be properly trained and learn respect and discipline. The Avenging Angels would see to it.

"It will be done, General." The friar bowed again.

Air displacement, the flapping of large wings, and a strange vibration made Konrad turn his head. He watched as a great tiger materialized in midair, flew down and alighted on the white marble floor. The beast carried a beautiful woman, and a wounded soldier across his back.

The friar gave the unusual tableau a perfunctory glance.

The tiger folded his wings, and the woman vaulted off the beast with the grace of a trained warrior. She wore pale blue armor above bare thighs, not the white angel uniform. She had bronzed skin, high cheek bones, and long flaxen braids loosely gathered into a top knot and falling back like a braided mane.

She leaned her bow and spear against the tiger's flank but still carried blades and profane blasters on her belt... like a walking arsenal. How odd for an angel. Not that her blasters would work here, where the abundance of Blue Crystal drained all conventional power sources.

Konrad also recognized her sword as a dragon fang– extremely rare and valuable.

He turned to the friar. "What kind of warrior angel is this woman? Why does she not wear the white uniform? This is a violation of the angel code!"

"Valka is not one of us, General... she just recruits for us." The friar's casual tone and nonchalant attitude grated on Konrad.

"Valka?" Konrad had never heard that name. And how did she penetrate the sacred enclave?

Healer angels in white robes, with a blue DNA helix on their sleeves, rushed forth, surrounding the tiger. They unloaded the wounded soldier on an antigrav pallet, then took him away.

Konrad noticed the glowing Blue Crystal powering the pallet, since profane technology didn't function on Byzantium.

When the beautiful woman turned and met his gaze, Konrad noticed her most fascinating feature, a pair of peridot-green eyes... not an angel, but a Zephyrian mind-reader... in warrior garb. He thought none of the Zephyrians survived the last witch hunt by the Priory, or the purge that followed.

Konrad touched the friar's sleeve. "If she's not an angel, why is she allowed inside the temple? This infraction smacks of sacrilege!"

The friar bowed, exposing his scalp markings. "She has her own powers, General, different but possibly greater than ours."

"Greater than ours?" Konrad scoffed at the very idea. Angels were the most powerful beings in the universe.

"She is also our best recruiter of worthy warriors for the great battle." The friar straightened, full of righteousness. "Worth every credit."

"She works for credits?" Konrad hated greedy mercenaries. "We shouldn't pay strangers to recruit new angels... no matter how efficient they are."

The friar scoffed and covered his bare skull with his hood. "We do what we can, General. But since the near destruction of Azura, the need is great, and the volunteers are few."

"How can that be?" Konrad didn't understand. "Who wouldn't want to become all powerful and quasi-immortal?"

The friar straightened and gave Konrad a disdainful glance. "Longevity tends to lose its appeal when you are headed for slaughter, General."

Konrad didn't want to cause an incident in this sacred place. "Of course..." Since the last evil entity was banished and had sworn to avenge his minions, the angels expected a bloody battle in the near future. "I understand and I apologize."

The friar nodded his forgiveness. "We are all being tested by these dangerous times, General."

"True." Konrad berated himself for thinking like an Avenging Angel. He was no longer one. He'd barely survived the near destruction of Azura. "Thank you for recruiting so diligently."

The friar joined his hands in thanks, folded his arms inside his wide sleeves, then turned, and shuffled away.

"I heard your comments about bounty hunters, and I resent them... whoever the hell you are!" The strong battle voice of the Zephyrian woman came as a surprise. She was taller up close, and raised a stubborn chin.

Konrad chose to ignore her profanity and rose to his full height. He pulled down his white military tunic but refused to salute a lowly mercenary. "General Konrad Lagarde, First Mate of the *Blue Phantom*."

"The angel ship?" Her piercing green eyes studied him. "I didn't know angels had generals... or last names, for that matter."

"They don't... usually." Why did he feel the need to explain himself to her? "But I was a general in the GTA before becoming an angel. I guess the rank and last name stuck as a sign of respect."

"I see... My name is Valka, and at the moment, I work for the Azurans because they pay me well." She adjusted the blasters and blades on her belt. "That's all you need to know."

Konrad eased his stance. Zephyrians could read minds. Was she reading his? No. He would be able to detect it. He needed to learn more about her. Could her unusual abilities present a danger to his kind? The last skirmish on Azura proved that evil entities could bestow supernatural powers, and angels weren't invincible anymore.

He felt compelled to evaluate her. "May I ask where you acquired the power to dematerialize?"

"No, you may not, General." An amused smile twitched her full lips.

He pointed at her belt buckle with a white crystal inset in the shape of three interlocked triangles. "I'm not familiar with this particular symbol."

"It's called a Valknut. It represents death in battle, the heart of the slain." She said it with reverence. "The most glorious end for any warrior."

"A little morbid if you ask me." Konrad hated cults, especially those that revered death. He'd seen too many totalitarian regimes thriving on human sacrifice and genocide. "A good soldier should focus on following orders and winning the battle, not dying. Angels fight evil forces, so we can live in the light."

"But, dying in battle is the most noble path to eternal bliss, General." That amused smile again.

"Forgive me if I don't agree. I've seen too many senseless deaths." More than he cared to recall. "I value strategy, order, and discipline. That's how battles are won."

"Then you might want to join the Priory." She emitted a derisive snort. "The Abbotts love order, discipline, and total control."

How dare she suggest treason? "The Priory and its Abbotts are just another faceless cult exploiting people's fears, to assert their authority and fill their pockets."

"Are they, now?" She chuckled, her hand caressing the hilt of her sword. "Why should I care?"

Konrad grunted. "Don't you dare make light of these cults. They are dangerous for all of us. I spent time with such people in my GTA days. I know what they are like..." He'd lived his entire youth in a tyrannical organization. "But I'm an angel now. I fight for the light, and I have changed."

"Have you?" She faced him squarely and stared him in the eyes. "You are still a boring stick-in-the-mud following the rules, even when they don't make sense." She widened her stance in defiance, and stuck both thumbs in her belt. "I value freedom, creative thinking, and independence."

Konrad felt challenged and took a deep breath. "And I believe rules make the universe safer. Rules build safety guards. Why is it so hard for people to understand?"

"Rules enslave people. Besides, the enemy never follows them, so why should we?" So much bravado in her voice. "No one tells me what to do."

"That's too bad." Konrad realized he enjoyed sparring with her and suppressed a smile. "The Avenging Angels could use a warrior of your caliber in the great battle."

"No, thanks. I don't do great battles anymore." She chuckled. "Nothing could convince me to submit to your stringent rules, not even your perfect, super-soldier physique, or your captivating blue eyes."

"What?" He struggled not to show his surprise.

She winked at him, then pivoted on her boot heel and ambled away. The soft blue light bounced off the short blades tucked into her boots as she walked. Then she snatched her bow and spear and vaulted upon the tiger's back.

The tiger stared at Konrad, then shook his big head and growled. *Stay away, puny angel.*

Konrad heard the tiger's voice in his mind and shuddered at the warning. So, the big cat was telepathic... and didn't like him one bit. Strange... animals usually liked angels.

The woman named Valka patted the tiger's neck, then the beast took flight, and vanished with the woman.

Konrad shook his head. He would definitely report that tiger and find out how Valka acquired such angel powers... since she wasn't one. He hoped it wasn't from an evil source.

Did she call him perfect and captivating? Konrad smiled inside as he raked his short black hair. He was intrigued. He hoped their paths would cross again. This fascinating creature dared challenge him, and made him feel like a much younger man... although angels never aged.

Chapter Two

Valka sat on a boulder where she had a view of the semi-wild park of lawns and bushes. Tall trees punctuated the grass, lined along a narrow stream. Overhead, the pink sky indicated it was almost sunset on this tranquil rural planet. A few lazy clouds promised morning rain. Birds sang in the trees... or it might be large bugs or frogs celebrating the crepuscule.

It must be summer or spring, as the balmy breeze carried the fragrance of the many bushes in full bloom that sprinkled the grassy areas. Valka had seen so many planets over the centuries, it didn't matter anymore. Since she'd lost her home, none of them appealed to her. Not even this lovely green orb.

She unwrapped their meal bartered at a neighboring farm. Sultan sniffed his food, a large roasted bird in a paper box, then he checked her sandwich for good measure... smoked meat and freshly baked bread with a tantalizing aroma of unfamiliar herbs and spices... and a large mug of local ale. This backwoods paradise hadn't yet learned the secrets of tasteless synthetic food.

"Sultan like bird better." The tiger gave her a head bump in thanks then settled on the lawn to enjoy his meal.

She glanced around to make sure no one suspicious spied on them. It should be safe enough, but sometimes people objected to a large tiger loose in a semi-public place... or a warrior walking around in battle armor with deadly weapons.

She ate and drank... alone as always, while Sultan devoured his large bird. Then she took off her boots and weapons belt and took a dip in the shallow river, while Sultan drank from it. Clean and refreshed, she sat against a tree trunk to enjoy the sunset.

She couldn't help but reminisce about the arrogant general she'd met on Byzantium. Why did she mention his captivating blue eyes and supersoldier physique? It was stupid and irresponsible... but she couldn't help it. He reminded her of someone... someone she thought she'd forgotten long ago.

The memory brought great sorrow. She didn't want to remember. Too much guilt, too much suffering. She couldn't face the terrible consequences of letting herself love. She took a deep breath and pushed away the painful memories.

The tiger interrupted his facetious grooming to lick her face. *"Forget general angel. Sultan not like general."*

"Are you reading my mind again?" Valka was not surprised at Sultan's intrusion, but his statement puzzled her. The tiger usually liked the angels. "What is it about General Lagarde you don't like, Sweetheart?"

"Bad general make Valka sad." The tiger brushed his head against her shoulder. *"Sultan never make Valka sad."*

"Are you jealous?" She chuckled and patted the strong, furry neck. She couldn't blame the cat for adoring her. He couldn't help it. "I love you, too, Sweetheart, and I know I can always count on you."

Men weren't as reliable... then again, Sultan had no choice. His mind was imprinted to love, obey, and protect her, no matter what.

As the tiger lay down by her feet, Valka felt suddenly cold. She shuddered as a vision came upon her. A strong warrior woman in a cage, wounded, at a slave market. Her next target. This one deserved to be saved. The vision showed her where and when to find her mark. She knew that place, she'd been there many times.

Sultan bumped her foot. *"Vision?"*

"Yes, Sweetheart." She patted the tiger then relaxed enjoying the peaceful evening. "Let's have some rest. We have another important job to do tomorrow."

Sultan snorted his agreement and spread his big frame on the grass, alongside her.

An instrument at her belt buzzed. Valka checked the screen. Another giant rock had popped up for sale. Exactly the kind she was looking for... expensive, but perfect. She freed the credits to solidify the acquisition and provided coordinates for the delivery. A very good day, indeed.

She lay down in the grass beside Sultan, and the tiger laid a possessive paw on her arm. She didn't mind. But Valka's gaze returned to the stars in the darkening purple sky. She could not sleep. The face of the handsome general kept flashing in her mind. He felt so familiar... although she'd never met him before... but it could never be.

* * *

General Konrad Lagarde stood on the observation deck of the *Blue Phantom*. Here, like on Byzantium, the bulkhead glowed blue with the power of the enormous Azuran Crystal growing at the heart of the ship. The crystal drive hummed so gently it purred, and the recycled air smelled like spring flowers.

Through the clear observation dome, he could see Byzantium, floating in space, an iridescent blue sphere like a beacon of light, with many ships anchored to its outer ring. And surrounding it, outside the shimmering shield, an army of glowing AI sentinels, floating in space, ready to charge and smite any trespassers or attackers.

Konrad walked toward the tall amazon with short blond hair, Graziella the Merciful, the *Blue Phantom's* Captain.

He saluted, clicking his heels. "Captain, the new recruits, enlisted on Byzantium, are now onboard. A hundred of them. Not enough, but our temples are actively recruiting. We'll find more."

"I know we will, General." Graziella the Merciful smiled.

"Many of the new warriors recruited are recovering from various injuries; as for the civilian volunteers, they are in desperate need of military training." Konrad straightened his tall frame. "They have much to learn."

"Thank you for the thorough report, General." Captain Graziella nodded. "But you don't have to be so formal in your approach. Your obsession with discipline makes the crew nervous. Remember that you now serve on a rescue ship."

Konrad couldn't hide his surprise. "I believe in discipline onboard, Captain."

"I know you do, but although the *Blue Phantom* was once a GTA destroyer, we do not observe military rule here." Her smile widened, softening her blue eyes and fair face. "You are new here, and as my first officer, I expect you to relax a little."

"Noted, Captain." Konrad sighed. "But without strict military rule, a soldier might lose his edge. There is a battle coming soon, and discipline is good for the soldier's soul."

Graziella the Merciful narrowed her eyes at him. "We are crew, not soldiers or Avenging Angels, General. We have angelic AIs to fight for us. On this ship, we are all angels, supporting Azura and Byzantium, but we do not follow their rules."

"But, Captain," he exclaimed out of turn. "What about respect for your authority?"

"My authority or yours will never be challenged on the *Blue Phantom*, General. Our crew is made of angels and angelic AIs. They all respect us and each other."

"Still..." Konrad struggled to keep from blurting his opinion again.

Captain Graziella straightened. "You seem to confuse authority with pomp and decorum, General. True authority does not need all that ceremony."

"Aye, Captain. I will try to remember that." Konrad resisted the temptation to shake his head, and bit his lip instead, to prevent a sharper comment.

Captain Graziella focused her gaze on the Byzantium Space Station floating in space several klicks away. "I know you will do your best, General. Thank you."

But Konrad knew better. Experience taught him there would always be dangers lurking in the corners. No matter how safe angels thought they were... and not just dangers from the outside... especially if they relaxed the rules in their own enclaves.

"Captain!" a feminine voice called overhead, filling the dome. "Transmission from our spy on Pandemonium."

"The *Blue Phantom* uses spies?" Konrad couldn't keep the shock from his voice.

Graziella the Merciful chuckled at his reaction. "Yes, General, we have spies."

How pedestrian of the *Blue Phantom.* And Pandemonium was a wretched den of iniquity, no place for the righteous. "Not angels, I presume. Angels cannot lie."

"On the contrary, General, angels make perfect spies." Captain Graziella gestured and a console rose from the deck in front of her. "They can make themselves invisible, and materialize through walls or bulkheads undetected. And since we can synchronize our minds, we can see everything our spy sees, from here in real time."

She waved her hand over the console, and 3D images from inside the illegal Pandemonium space station appeared in the center of the dome.

Konrad braced himself. He'd never been on Pandemonium and didn't relish partaking of that mental experience.

* * *

Lord Zethar, owner and administrator of Pandemonium, hated the Priory and its Abbotts, with their black robes, masked faces, gold medallions, and dark secrets. They fancied themselves as the only righteous order, and the future rulers of the universe.

So, when three of them requested an audience and boarded his clandestine and always moving space station, Zethar wondered how they found it. They must have connections deep in the lowest layers of society. He expected trouble.

From his hidden office, He watched them on the clear wall of security monitors lining the bulkhead. They walked slowly through the populated avenues of the slums, surrounded by a red mist, and followed by a dozen fully armed robotic soldiers. No brains, just black armor and absolute obedience programming. The three Abbotts in black hats and robes, concealing their faces behind a mask, nodded right and left, probably enjoying the fear they imparted in everyone.

Many residents kneeled or prostrated themselves along the way. Even the toughest criminals of Pandemonium bowed to them out of fear, while others scrambled away to hide at their approach.

But Zethar had worked too hard to become the most powerful crime lord of this quadrant, to be intimidated by the dramatic displays of power-hungry Abbotts. He was a shrewd ruler in his own right. With the electronic hard and software in his brain, he mentally turned off the entire wall of security monitors above. The unwelcome visitors didn't need to see what took place in his illegal trading and gambling emporium.

Zethar checked himself in the reflective surface of a dark screen and smoothed his shiny skull plates. He was ready.

As his office door opened, Zethar displayed his most charming smile and rose to his intimidating height, taller than any Human. He could see over the Abbotts' faceless heads, despite their high shoes and tall head dresses. The red mist surrounding them receded, and the three masked figures stood facing him, very straight, as if expecting him to salute or bow to them.

Zethar refused to show them any kind of deference. Not a chance. He served no one, not even the mighty angels he helped on occasion in exchange for credits or technology—like the invisible spy he'd invited to witness this audience. It bothered him a little that he couldn't see her, but the angels would make strong allies... just in case the Abbotts decided to turn against him.

"Your Graces... what a rare honor to receive representatives of the Priory." Zethar indicated three chairs facing his desk. "Please, sit."

The Abbotts looked at each other's black masks but didn't speak. They hesitated then sat on the chairs, while the robotic guards stood behind them like metallic chess pieces.

Zethar took his higher seat behind his desk, looking down on them. He hoped they couldn't detect the angel spy in the room. But hell, if he couldn't, they probably couldn't either. "What can I do for Your Graces?"

It seemed for a few seconds that the Abbotts were communicating, but not with sound or sign language. Zethar suspected they used private mind-speech technology. He focused on their thoughts, but could not read their minds. They used some kind of neural shielding to block his tech from reading them. Fark!

The middle Abbott straightened in his chair. "Lord Zethar, we would like the privilege to use your special market to do some trade."

The distorted voice through the privacy sound system sounded impersonal, neither male nor female, electronic in nature. These Abbotts were paranoid about being identified. One could do all sorts of mischief hiding behind a mask, with no fear of repercussions.

"You mean to use my illegal slave market to sell your prisoners?" Zethar resisted the urge to smile. "That's going to cost you, Your Graces. A thousand credits per market day, and eighty percent of every sale."

The three Abbotts gasped all at once. The robotic guards straightened, right hand on their blasters. Zethar focused his mind on the hidden guns in the bulkhead and poised them on the guards. At any sudden move, he could fire the guns with one thought.

"Eighty percent?" The middle Abbott tsked. "My son, you should realize it is a great honor to serve us, and there are advantages to being in our good graces."

"I do. But you should realize that if the galaxy at large knew you were dealing in the illegal slave trade, you would lose the support of many major planets."

"Lord Zethar..." The patronizing tone through the electronic distortion still held reproach. "We were told we could count on your discretion."

"You can. Absolutely." Zethar smiled wide. "But discretion and security do not come cheap. The same way you maintain your Cyborg and robotic army, I have to maintain my private mercenary force, on this station and on my planets."

"But can't you make an exception? Be more accommodating to the Priory?" The electronic voice brimmed with mind-controlling vibes. "It might be to your advantage. We are very powerful."

"I know." Zethar resisted the urge to wince. Good thing his brain shield protected him from thought controlling devices. "But I am also a powerful man. And it's very friendly of me to allow you access to my market." He pursed his lips in concentration. "Besides, if it became known that I lowered my fees for anyone at all, I could lose my hard-earned reputation as a shrewd businessman."

"But what about your soul, my son?" The electronic tone now dripped with honeyed hypocrisy.

Zethar chuckled. "Did you take a good look at me through your black masks, Lord Abbotts? I rule the underbelly of this entire quadrant, and my body is more metal than flesh. I exchanged my soul for technology a long time ago. Do not preach to me about salvation. Such beliefs are for the weak and the gullible. You of all people should know that, since you are experts in selling such lies."

The middle Abbott straightened in his chair, as if offended. "The Priory improves lives everywhere by adding a spiritual dimension to this galaxy, my son."

"No, you don't. You enslave and exploit people for your own profit." Zethar hardened his voice. "And I'm not your son... although, we do share a taste for the mighty credits."

The three Abbotts gasped. The robotic guards remained still. Did they detect the many hidden guns poised on them? It didn't matter.

The Abbott in the middle cleared his throat. "You put us in a difficult position, my son." A hint of desperation colored the electronic voice. "Maybe we can still come to a better arrangement on the price?"

"Unless it's better for me, not a chance." Zethar grinned. These Abbotts seemed in a bind. An unusual thing for them. "So, when should I expect your first arrival of merchandise?"

The middle Abbott emitted a deep sigh. "Early tomorrow for the morning's market."

"Perfect." Zethar knew they had no other choice. He was their only slave market option in this quadrant. "I expect to be paid in credits in advance for the fee, and promptly, after each transaction for my eighty percents... or else..."

"Of course, Lord Zethar, of course." So much resentment and chagrin in the electronic voice.

Then, the Abbotts rose and left his office with great ceremony and Zethar watched them leave. Then he locked the doors and turned on the circular flexglaz wall of monitors.

The female angel spy rematerialized at his side, impeccable in her white uniform. She smiled and bowed to him. "Thank you, Lord Zethar, for helping a good cause. Your assistance is greatly appreciated and will be rewarded."

Then the angel woman deployed her wings, hovered above the deck, and vanished again.

Zethar rejoiced. This was a good day. The angels always kept their word, and they would reward him generously in angel technology for being privy to this edifying meeting... also, he would make a substantial profit from tomorrow's added sales.

* * *

Konrad couldn't believe the scene he'd just witnessed on the hologram. The Priory seeking the services of the underbelly of society? Making an alliance with a powerful crime lord? "This request from the Abbotts is worrisome."

"I agree." Graziella the Merciful closed her eyes as she spoke to the angel spy on Pandemonium. "Excellent job. Follow the Abbotts back to their headquarters on Taurus Secundus, and gather as much information as you can. I want to know why they changed their tactics and what they are plotting."

"Aye, aye, Captain." The feminine voice of the angel spy filled the dome. "I'll keep you posted."

"You are sending an angel inside a Priory stronghold?" Konrad shrugged off the disgust crawling on his skin at the very thought.

"Yes, of course. We get our information from the source. How else can we be certain?" Captain Graziella didn't seem troubled at all by this unorthodox method.

Konrad shook his head, trying to cope. "Although I do not approve of the means, Captain, I must admit that inside information would be most valuable... especially since the Abbotts have been expanding their aggressive agenda at an unprecedented rate."

"I'm glad you finally see the advantage of angel spies, General." Captain Graziella waved and the console shrank down and disappeared into the deck. "So far, the Priory's spiritual influence and their military oppression remains limited to a few star systems. It does not threaten the balance of good and evil in the rest of the galaxy."

Konrad nodded his understanding. "The fact that they would seek support from the most infamous crime lord in the quadrant, however, indicates they could be planning something bigger... and underhanded."

"My thoughts exactly." Captain Graziella rubbed her chin. "I fear this might be a clue that the same evil we banished cycles ago has risen again, and could be using the Abbotts as a vessel for a galaxy-wide conquest."

"That's a big jump to conclusions." But it had happened before, and Konrad tended to agree. "It would catch us unprepared. The angels are not ready for another great battle."

"Not yet." Graziella sighed. "It would be a disaster."

Konrad realized the dangers. "But how can the Priory afford the cost of such an extensive crusade?"

"That's what we need to discover." Captain Graziella narrowed her clear blue eyes at him. "We need boots on the deck of that Pandemonium slave market in the morning."

"Are you asking me to spy?" Konrad couldn't help the surprise choking his voice.

"Of course not, General. You are a soldier, not a spy. You would be terrible at it." Graziella chuckled. "I need you to officially contact Lord Zethar in person, and get his take on the Abbotts. Besides, it will do you some good to see the underbelly of civilization for yourself... not from the protected heights of the High Council. You are not on Azura anymore. The *Blue Phantom* roams the real galaxy."

"Aye, aye, Captain." Konrad straightened and refrained from pointing out that thousands of angels died and Azura was nearly destroyed in the last battle. "As you said, I'm a soldier. I follow orders, even if I don't like the mission."

"That's all right if you don't like my orders, General." Graziella the Merciful straightened and looked straight into his soul. "I know I can count on your sense of duty."

"Right. Of course you can, Captain." Sometimes Konrad wished angels could lie.

As he walked off the observation dome, along the glowing corridors of the ship, Konrad feared his captain didn't realize how fast a new galactic power could rise. He had seen political greed up close and knew how such empires operated in the shadows before emerging in full force. He'd once commanded large armies for such a power. He shuddered at the recollection of his time in the GTA.

But he also knew that such leaders were fickle, often dishonest, and always opportunistic. He'd been wronged and betrayed and had worn the scars of standing up for righteousness for many cycles. He chuckled. His mortal enemy had paid the ultimate price... but not before Konrad scarred him back, exposing his shame.

As for Konrad, thanks to the fact that angels had incomparable healing abilities, no physical scar remained on his body, but the same couldn't be said about his psyche.

* * *

Back in his Spartan quarters on the *Blue Phantom*, Konrad relaxed a little before tomorrow's mission. He lay on his bunk, eyes fixed to the white bulkhead. His mind reminisced about the mysterious creature he'd met this morning. Valka... the gorgeous warrior with fascinating green eyes, who wore a Valknut belt buckle and flew on a genetically enhanced tiger.

A very protective beast, that tiger. He growled at Konrad, baring his fangs, and told him to stay away from his mistress. Strange cat. Animals usually loved the energy flowing around the angels.

It bothered him that Valka had many angel powers but wasn't one. It also bothered him that he found her intriguing, to the point that he couldn't stop thinking about her. He'd never met a woman who could capture his attention like her. He hated the distraction, but the very thought of her strong silhouette and stubborn chin made him smile.

He needed to find out what she was... other than a bounty hunter and a Zephyrian mind-reader. He must make certain she wasn't a threat to his kind. So, he sat in midair and linked his mind to the Akashic vault containing the entire knowledge of the universe.

Then he focused on the strange crystal symbol on her belt. Three interlocked triangles, or pyramids. She called it a Valknut.

Ancient history unfolded on his mind's screen, of a defunct planet called Asgard. The Valknut was a symbol of the Valkyries, superhuman women warriors with strong powers. They flew over the battlefield on winged horses or swans, and collected the souls of valorous fighters, guiding them to the ever-feasting halls of Valhalla. Although sometimes, they elected to save their lives instead.

According to the Akashic records, they wielded a dragon fang blade, and the connection to their power resided mainly in their armor. But the last Valkyries perished during the battle of Ragnarök, which destroyed their home planet... although a few may have been too far out in the universe to hear the call to arms, and could have missed the final battle.

Since this battle took place a few millennia ago, it meant that, among other powers, the Valkyries also had angel-like longevity.

Konrad opened his eyes and lowered himself to sit on his sleeping bunk. A surviving Valkyrie would explain a lot... except that Valka was obviously a Zephyrian... another extinct race. This mystery was far from solved.

Chapter Three

As Valka strode along the main thoroughfare of Pandemonium with Sultan at her side, people stared. But in such a place, no one cared what she was and she didn't have to hide. On each side, displays and shops advertised illegal contraband, stolen goods, the latest designer drugs, weapons, the newest technology for robbers and marauders of all calibers.

"Bad people here." The tiger sounded irritated in her head.

"I know, we are gathering a lot of attention, Sweetheart." She patted the big beast. "But no one will dare attack us, and we can vanish anytime. Besides, we want to be seen by our targets as benevolent saviors who do not hide."

Valka shuddered at the shifty crowd of thieves and pickpockets. Not a worthy soul in the lot. She closed her mind to their murky intruding thoughts. A short man stopped in front of her. He unfolded a rolled leather bag and displayed an arsenal of blades for sale. Nothing good. She shrugged him off and kept walking.

The smell of roasting rat meat and fried giblets didn't bother Valka as much as the large screens above, displaying gladiator games, pitting big cats against other animals, or cats against defenseless humans, or alien monsters with teeth made of metal, mangling and shredding their victims. There was no honor in such fights.

"Sultan not like Pandemonium." Despite his impressive size, strength, and brutality in battle, he had the heart of a big softie.

"Neither do I." Valka turned her head from the carnage in disgust. What people did to each other for entertainment and gain bothered her.

She hated Pandemonium, but the slave market was a good place to recruit for the angels and her vision guided her here. She didn't have any qualms about stealing from the slave traders. Most of the warriors for sale were bound for the bloody games anyway, and she enjoyed giving them a chance at another kind of life... no matter how short... and an honorable death for a high purpose.

A tall, greasy man in a long fur coat stepped in front of her, brandishing a credit stick. "How much for the tiger?"

Sultan snorted in warning, but the ruffian didn't seem to care.

Valka spotted the man's accomplice watching from a safe distance. "Sultan is not for sale."

The tiger growled. *"Sultan not like man."*

The tall man grabbed Valka's arm. "I do insist, lady. Everything has a price."

Sultan roared, baring his fangs.

"Calm down, Sweetheart." She said in his mind.

The tiger grunted and lowered his head in obedience. Good.

"Not everything is for sale." She grasped the man's arm and twisted it. Then she hooked his leg and lowered her center of gravity. As he lost his balance, she slid under him, then sprang up, sending the man flying high before he dropped and kissed the deck... hard.

A jolt of electricity hit Valka when his accomplice shot her with a high voltage stun gun. But her armor absorbed most of the shock, and thanks to her special constitution, she didn't even flinch. In a flash, she threw a short blade that buried smack in the middle of the shooter's forehead. As he fell like a log, the first aggressor found his legs and stood up.

But Sultan now faced the ruffian, blocking his path, and roared, staring into the man's fearful eyes.

There was no law enforcement on Pandemonium, only survival of the fittest. But Valka didn't want to draw attention from Zethar's private security. The ruffian had learned his lesson. "Sultan, let him go."

The tiger desisted with a snort and a shake of his big head.

The tall ruffian ran away as fast as he could on his long legs. No one among the thieves and degenerates loitering around seemed to take offense, or even notice. They were too busy liberating the dead man of his belongings.

Soon Valka and Sultan reached the crowded marketplace. Valka closed her eyes briefly and remembered her vision of a valorous woman warrior, wounded but still for sale, probably destined for the disgusting games in the arena. Although this wasn't a battlefield, there still remained the aftermath of battle. Valka would always fulfill her duty to worthy warriors.

She straightened as she sensed the discordant vibrations of an ominous presence, hidden but powerful... watching the market from the shadows. Someone with dark purpose and an even darker soul. Valka shuddered as she recognized the unholy vibe. She'd felt it before, in the presence of high officers of the sect called the Priory... those scary black figures without faces. An Abbott of the Priory here? On Pandemonium? How surprising.

Valka shouldn't care. Politics didn't concern her. Yet, she couldn't help the revulsion at the very thought of the dark order. And what were they doing in this rat-infested gambling hell? Nothing good, for sure.

As she ambled along the rows of cages, looking for the worthy warrior of her vision, she steeled herself. She wished she could free all these children, animals, men and women bound for a life of suffering or hard labor. But she couldn't. She wasn't powerful enough to save the entire galaxy. The universe was broken, and she did her best to restore the balance by rescuing warriors for the final battle, one at a time.

The face of the handsome general with deep blue eyes she'd met the day before on the angel space station flashed upon her mind. She sensed his presence. What was the first mate of the *Blue Phantom* doing in such a horrible place?

For some reason, he reminded her of the only man she ever loved. Her heart skipped a beat, and her chest filled with something akin to happiness. Something she hadn't felt in a thousand cycles. But she quickly checked herself. Romantic attraction was a trap. She'd laid down her armor for love once, and it cost her everything.

Never again.

* * *

As he made his way across the slave market, Konrad felt out of place in his white angel uniform. He shuddered at the spectacle of people and animals in cages or in chains, head down, sad, hopeless. The light emanating from their bodies almost nonexistent, compared to the luminous aura of angels.

Of course, most of the merchants and buyers here couldn't see auras, so preoccupied with their greed and petty problems. None of them noticed the glow from the energy pervading all life.

Konrad held his breath against the disgusting stench of unwashed bodies, lousy recycled air, and roasting meat... not the lab-grown protein packs, but probably the victims of the games. How could people eat dead animals? Or worse... But he'd once been a meat eater, too. At the time, it smelled and tasted good. Not anymore. His long sojourn on Azura had forever changed his views on many things.

Still, he wished he could smite all these evil doers, free all these victims of war and greed... destroy this wicked place. But evil had its place in the universe. It was even necessary. Besides, his captain sent him to Pandemonium to gather information as an observer... another word for spy. He hated this mission.

He didn't relish meeting Lord Zethar, who ruled Pandemonium. The man had been friendly to angels in the past, but Konrad had no illusion. The crime lord only had his own interest at heart.

A cold draft raised the small hair on Konrad's nape. Abbotts of the Priory were here, hidden, watching, keeping an eye on their illegal merchandise. He could feel their disturbing presence nearby. He hoped they didn't have powers of invisibility.

Then Konrad spotted an unexpected silhouette in the crowd coming toward him, and his heartbeat quickened. A fierce woman warrior with bronzed skin and flaxen braids, walking alongside a majestic tiger. For some reason, he didn't hate this mission quite as much as he had moments ago.

Valka stopped a few paces from him, and the large tiger sat at her side, growling and baring his teeth.

A pleasurable frisson coursed along his spine as Konrad closed the gap. He couldn't keep the grin from his face. But what was she doing here?

She stared straight at him with those fascinating peridot green eyes and smiled. "General Konrad Lagarde, are you following me? This doesn't feel like a proper place for someone like you."

"Sultan not like Angel Konrad." The tiger rose menacingly then turned and rubbed his head against Valka's shoulder. Then the beast sat back and licked his paw but kept an eye on Konrad. *"Stay away, Angel Konrad."*

Valka patted the cat's head. "Be nice Sultan. The general is our friend."

Konrad forced a smile. "Nice to meet you, too, Sultan. But I am not your enemy."

So, the tiger could mind-talk and had mind-reading abilities as well. Konrad focused on Valka. He didn't know how to act around her. He didn't want to like her. "I have more important things to do than follow a credit hungry hunter."

Her smile vanished and her green gaze could cut glass. "What makes you so perfect, General? I'd bet you have a few skeletons in your angel closet. Remember, the mighty always fall... even angels."

"True." Konrad couldn't believe she would utter such words to an angel, but she was right. His fear of liking her made him aggressive. He took a deep breath to calm his mind. "What are you doing in this dreary place?"

She shrugged. "I go wherever the visions lead me, but that's none of your business."

"Visions?" Such abilities in non-angel hands might endanger his kind. "You can see the future?"

"I'm not a fortune teller." She shook her head and frowned. "I see the souls of worthy warriors... in great danger of dying."

Konrad remembered his research on the Valkyries flying over the cold battlefield. "Where do your visions come from? Who is sending them to you?"

"You ask too many questions, General." Valka straightened, as if to leave. "Remember, curiosity killed the cat."

Was that an open threat? How dare she?

Sultan shook himself and growled in protest. *"Sultan strong. Not die."*

Valka pursed her lips and scratched the big cat's chin. "Of course not, Sweetheart."

Konrad relaxed a little. "Well, I have business to conduct. But I'm sure we'll meet again, Valka."

"Careful what you wish, General." She chuckled and walked away with Sultan, in the direction of the cages lined up in front of the Arena.

Did she intend to steal slaves and resell them to the Azurans? Konrad hoped not. That could complicate his dealings with Lord Zethar. Although, since Valka was an independent bounty hunter, the angels couldn't be held responsible for her behavior.

Still... Konrad hated himself for excusing her in his mind. Everything about her threatened his righteousness. But she had a point. Angels shouldn't get involved in politics or have dealings with shady crime lords... or beautiful bounty hunters.

Konrad also wondered what kind of entity was sending visions to Valka, since Asgard was destroyed and Odin was long dead. This kind of power always had a source. For the angels, it was the Blue Crystal linked to the Formless One... but other sources included various gods or powerful entities, some benevolent, others mischievous, and some dangerously evil.

So many unknown forces in the universe could threaten the balance of light and darkness at any time. Although, Konrad never felt darkness inside Valka, only defiance in her stubborn stance and fascinating green eyes.

As Konrad walked toward the elevator to the station's Command Center, his gaze stopped on the lanky figure of Lord Zethar himself, waiting for the elevator, giving orders to a subaltern. Taller than any man, and recognizable by the fancy red, gold, and silver plates covering his skull, Zethar wore a long fur coat and fine leather boots. Animal skins... how repulsive.

Konrad directed his steps toward the crime lord. Time to do his duty. Zethar may not be easy to convince. But if the Priory was on the verge of a galactic invasion, the angels would need all the help they could get.

* * *

As Valka neared Warrior Row in the slave market, where larger cages lined the front entrance of the Arena, she recognized the place of her vision. More than the sight, it was the stink of despair, the powerful scent of the menagerie close-by, the proximity of death, the dirt and grime, and the sound of steel bars closing on the unfortunate.

Sultan, shuffling alongside her, seemed uneasy. *"Sultan not like bad station."*

"Me neither, Sweetheart, but we have a warrior to save."

Over the millennia, Valka's visions never misled her. They never lied. The female warrior was close. Valka could sense her stubborn lifeforce, her agony, her refusal to die despite nasty wounds... and her will to escape. Good. Definitely a worthy soul.

Valka's gaze searched for her among all these warriors and other prisoners destined for the games. So many of them, even children and animals.

She sensed the disturbing vibe of the Abbotts again. Were they here to trade? Was that how they generated revenue to finance their military campaigns? Did they sell lives to buy killing machines and soulless robots, who didn't need to get paid or fed, weren't afraid to die, and would never question an order?

This was so wrong. But Valka obeyed no one, and didn't abide by anyone's rules. She had the freedom to decide who to save. Today, she would save the worthy warrior woman of her vision... if the woman agreed to fight in the final battle.

Chapter Four

As he followed the half-robotic crime lord inside the Command Center of Pandemonium, General Konrad Lagarde shivered. This horrible station was no place for an angel. It felt as if the cold touch of evil had landed on his shoulder and lingered there. The foul smell of unwashed bodies and hot grease improved slightly inside the Command Center, but not much. At least the floor was clean.

Konrad controlled his revulsion but couldn't fake a smile. "Lord Zethar, thank you for allowing our agent to witness and transmit your meeting with the Abbotts of the Priory."

Konrad gazed up at the circular flexglaz wall above, showing images of various parts of Pandemonium. From here, the crime lord could see everything happening in his space station, from the main thoroughfare and its shops to the Arena, the marketplace, as well as the gambling dens, the Menagerie, the security headquarters, and various corridors with their nooks and crannies.

Lord Zethar grinned and indicated the monitors with a wide wave of his hand. "All this, and I can control the entire security system with the interactive software implanted in my brain."

"Impressive." Konrad had no doubt the man could. He had many abilities... thanks to the advances of science, and stolen technology.

Lord Zethar pointed to a seat for Konrad. "Always glad to oblige the angels safeguarding the galaxy. But you must understand my services always come at a price."

"I understand perfectly. And you will be paid." Konrad bit his lips to prevent a sharper comment, then sat in the offered chair.

Lord Zethar took the higher seat behind his desk. "I prefer to be paid in Azuran technology rather than credits."

"Straight to the point." Konrad didn't agree with disseminating angel tech, but the fate of the galaxy might depend on him obtaining information. Besides, he had his orders to win over the crime lord at any cost. His face, however, still refused to smile. "Depending on the value of your help, I'm sure it can be arranged."

"Good." Lord Zethar relaxed against the back of his chair and shuffled a few small items on his desk. "As you can see, I'm a collector of valuable angel artifacts."

"I see." Konrad recognized some of these gadgets as angel tech and remembered they contained tiny amounts of Blue Crystal. And Blue Crystal had many properties... An idea started to form in his mind. "How long have you owned these?"

"Since the last skirmish with evil, two cycles ago. I used to have more, but some got lost." The crime lord smiled and looked perfectly relaxed.

"Lost?" Konrad raised an eyebrow at the blatant lie. Although some electronic interference prevented him from reading Zethar's mind, he had no doubt the missing artifacts had been sold to the highest bidders, with no concern about how they might be used. Although these were not weapons, they could be adapted to threaten angel security.

"Have you come to my station to insult me General?" Lord Zethar straightened his back. "Or do you have legitimate business to conduct with me?"

"Sorry." Konrad would have to control his gut reactions. He was never cut out to be a spy. "It seems the Abbotts of the Priory are preparing to expand their military campaigns on a dangerously larger scale."

The crime Lord narrowed his dark eyes on Konrad. "That's what it looks like to me, too. All the signs are there. In the last cycle, they have been liquidating their assets and ordering more robotic warriors... in exceedingly large numbers."

"We gathered the same information." Konrad wished he could read the man's mind. Damn the electronic interference that prevented him from doing so.

"So, you have your own sources. Why do you need me?" Zethar played hard to get.

"We suspect their increased confidence might come from a new benefactor, who is giving them the means to influence others with more than credits or religious ideas." Konrad shuddered. He remembered the same aura of evil and mystery from his experience in the GTA, when the leaders made secret pacts with dark forces. It still affected him, although it happened long ago.

The crime lord shook his metal-plated head. "You mean they recourse to some kind of mind-binding sorcery?"

"It's one explanation for their sudden change of tactics and daring methods." In Konrad's experience new power made ambitious men bolder.

Zethar chuckled. "Well, they did try to influence my judgement during the meeting. Fortunately, my mind is electronically protected from such interference."

Konrad remembered Captain Graziella mentioning Zethar's involvement in the last angel skirmish with evil. "Do you have reason to believe the Abbotts are practicing any kind of black magic rituals?"

"I hear many rumors, General, but most are baseless, only born of fear." The man rose from his chair. "I hate black magic. It often uses bloody rituals. But I wouldn't be surprised if the Abbotts practiced it. Their gruesome theatricals give me the creeps. They thrive on generating fear. It's their strongest weapon."

"Many sects and authoritarian groups sustain their power through fear." Konrad searched for a reaction in the tin man's face but saw none. "From the new vibrations surrounding the Abbotts, we suspect their benefactor might be an evil entity from outside this galaxy."

Zethar grimaced, as if remembering something disturbing. "I had a brush with a minion of such an entity a while back, and I didn't care for it." The tin man looked in the distance. "Do you know for a fact such a force is involved?"

"The last evil entity we expelled from this universe almost destroyed us." Konrad remembered it well. He barely survived the near obliteration of Azura. "That evil being promised to return and destroy all angels."

"Great!" Lord Zethar stopped pacing and turned to face Konrad. "How does that concern me? I am not an angel. And I'm sure you have a plan to stop it."

Konrad took a deep breath and straightened in his chair. "We do have a plan, but we need your help. You have many connections in the sordid corners of the hidden world."

Zethar grinned. "Lucky for you, I do. As long as you are prepared to provide me with the kind of payment I need."

"What do you hope to get from us?" The very idea made Konrad cringe.

Zethar straightened his tall frame and locked his hands behind his back. "My goal is to acquire all the powers of an angel and become immortal."

Konrad gasped. "That's all?" How he hated dealing with Zethar. "Angelhood comes with many obligations, Lord Zethar. We obey the Formless One, we work only for the greater good, our hearts are pure, and we do not lie. Also, we are not immortal, angels can be killed."

"Still, if I'm not an angel, and only possess the powers of one, I have none of your obligations. I can live forever, profiting from my illegal trades, and no one will be able to thwart me..." Zethar stared at a particular screen on the circular wall above and narrowed his eyes.

Konrad glanced up at the impressive display of surveillance screens. "What is it?"

"This irritating female and her cat, again. She's been stealing wounded warriors from my slave market with impunity. Somehow, she always vanishes before my security team can catch her. But not this time." Zethar touched his skull plate and froze, as if giving mental orders.

"Stolen warriors?" Could it be Valka and her tiger? Konrad struggled with his inability to read the crime lord's mind. How disconcerting.

When he located the right screen, his heart skipped a beat as he did recognize the female in question. Valka and her tiger, checking the cages near the Arena. Konrad had guessed right. Valka stole slaves from the most powerful crime lord in the quadrant and sold them to the Azurans, implicating Azura in criminal activities. How brazen... and inconvenient. It was so wrong on so many levels and could compromise his mission.

Angels should never get involved with criminals. And it seemed Valka was just as crooked and greedy as the common bounty hunter scum. The very notion pinched something in Konrad's chest.

* * *

On warrior row of the slave market, where cages lined the wall along the Arena, Valka spotted from a distance the wounded female of her vision. She lay on the metallic floor plate of her cage, too severely injured to sit or stand. As Valka attempted to read the woman's mind, she could not. The poor soul must be unconscious.

"Sultan see warrior." The tiger snorted and loped ahead.

Valka hated slave traffickers and enjoyed stealing from them. A shame that in this day and age, no one cared enough to provide basic first aid for these unfortunate prisoners. The traders treated them like garbage. Didn't they understand that better health would increase the value of their merchandise?

No civilian buyers loitered around warrior row. No surprise there. They preferred docile slaves, especially the females. But in the arena, a woman warrior always garnered larger bets than males, and her suffering spoke to a wider audience. How disgusting.

The game sponsors usually swooped in at the end of the market and bought wounded warriors at rock-bottom prices. They would make them fight as gladiators if they were able. If not, the unlucky would fend for their lives in desperation, in a public display, against the infernal beasts unleashed to devour them.

Sultan sniffed around the cage with open interest. *"Funny smell."*

"Must be the blood and unwashed bodies." As she drew closer, Valka could see the woman, still wearing armor, but no weapons. The bloody bandages around her thigh smelled ripe. Infection was spreading. The poor soul didn't have long to live. The cage door was ajar. Not locked. Strange... even though the prisoner wasn't in any condition to escape.

No matter. Instead of materializing inside, Valka pulled open the door and walked into the cage.

Sultan followed her. *"Funny smell... strong."*

"I only smell blood and putrefaction." Valka looked around the cage but saw nothing out of the ordinary.

"No, not blood." The tiger sniffed the air. *"Smell like angel."*

"There is no angel here." Although, she'd seen the general in the market. Valka knelt by the unconscious woman. "Hey! Wake up. Talk to me."

Sultan licked the woman's face. No reaction.

Valka checked for a pulse at the wrist. She felt a faint heartbeat... still alive, but barely. An unconscious warrior, however, would never do. She needed the woman's informed consent to save and recruit her for the great battle. The dying warrior must be given a choice.

Otherwise, Valka might as well be another despicable slave trader. Although worldly rules didn't matter much to her kind, this one was sacred, and unbreakable.

Sultan hissed. *"Bad people come."*

The cage door slammed closed and locked on its own. Soldiers in black military armor swarmed from every direction and pointed their blasters at the cage. How ridiculous! They couldn't stop Valka. No cage could hold her.

Sultan crouched low and emitted a menacing growl.

"Easy, Sweetheart. These are just underlings." She loaded her prized warrior on Sultan. "No space to deploy your wings, but that's okay."

No matter. She focused her mind on a safe place where the woman could be treated and give her consent. Since General Konrad Lagarde was on station for business, the *Blue*

Phantom must be close by. Valka might even have stolen an image of the inside of his ship from his unsuspecting mind.

Focusing on the angel ship, Valka mentally dematerialized the three of them.

Nothing happened. What?

Baffled, she tried again. No luck. Why did her abilities fail her? Was she no longer worthy? What happened? Cold tendrils of fear snaked down her back.

By now, the cage was surrounded by black armored soldiers who kept their distance as the cage floated off the deck. They were quiet, efficient. Highly trained. Mercenaries, no doubt. Valka slid down from Sultan, unloaded the unconscious warrior woman and grabbed the bars for balance.

"Hey!" She called to the closest soldier. "Where are you taking us?"

The black-armored man walking alongside the cage didn't even seem to hear her.

Focusing on him to read his mind about his orders, Valka realized she couldn't. She threw a short blade aimed at his neck through the bars to get his attention, but it sizzled and bounced off an invisible shield around the cage. How was this possible?

What kind of trap was this? Who had the technology to neutralize her abilities? No cage had ever held Valka before. What could she do? Her chest felt cold inside.

The last time Valka felt so helpless was when she laid down her armor for the love of a man... and lost her powers while her realm was reduced to ashes... and all her sisters were slain. Chills ran up her spine at the painful memory.

Then she wondered why the general reminded her so much of the man she once loved... could it be him? No. Impossible. He'd died long ago... although...

A small door in the Arena wall ahead lifted open with a whoosh of compressed air. Valka's cage floated into a dark, stinky space, full of other cages in tight rows. Moans of pain and fear from people and animals reached her ears. The Menagerie!

Images of bloody combat in the Arena flashed through her mind. The fights were rigged. No one ever won. Valka had never feared for her life until now. What could she do?

* * *

Konrad struggled to hide his apprehension as he stepped into the Menagerie with Zethar and his bodyguards. The stench of wild beasts, putrefaction, blood, and urine made him want to wretch.

Zethar laughed as they walked along the rows of cages. "Come see Azuran technology at work. I adapted the angel tech I gained from the last skirmish with evil to create cages to trap beings with supernatural abilities."

Konrad suppressed a grunt. The angels should never have given such technology to a crime lord, no matter how helpful. Zethar could neutralize, catch, and hold angels with this device. It was a threat to angel kind.

Animal whimpers and prisoners' moans reached Konrad's ears. What a terrible place. What shameful treatment of sentient creatures. As they approached Valka's cage, Konrad bit his lips in frustration. Despite all her infractions and irritating qualities, he still wanted to help her.

Valka planted her fists on her hips in challenge.

The tiger growled menacingly and snarled at Konrad. Definitely not friendly.

On the cage floor, a woman warrior in full armor, with a rotting leg wound, lay unconscious.

Konrad had never before found himself in such a conundrum. Angels never lied. If asked directly, he would have to admit Azura's connection with Valka. Worse, he wanted her to escape this horrible place... along with all the prisoners in the Menagerie.

Zethar grinned. "So, little lady, you thought you and your feline companion could steal from my slave market without consequences?"

Valka snorted. "Your market is illegal. You don't own these people. Every single one of them was stolen anyway. Who did you pay off to operate this station without hindrance? Do you get protection from the Abbotts? I felt their creepy vibes. They are here, aren't they?"

Konrad had felt them, too. But he knew they only kept an eye on the slave market to protect their financial interests.

Lord Zethar straightened his tall frame. "I do not need any protection, little lady. I am a force to reckon with. I own this space station and several planets in this quadrant, and I have my own army to protect my dominions. I fear no one."

"Not even the angels?" Valka shot Konrad an accusing stare. "And you! How can you deal with such filth? You are sullying the reputation of all angels! Shame on you, General!"

Zethar cast Konrad an intrigued glance. "How does she know who and what you are? Do you know each other?"

Konrad gasped. How dare she involve him?

"No, we don't know each other." Valka smirked. "But unlike most, I can sense angel powers, and I can see their light. Besides, the white uniform, the blue eyes, and the more than perfect physique, all are dead giveaways. And from my vast knowledge, sensing the *Blue Phantom* in the vicinity, I deduced that he must be General Konrad Lagarde, First Mate of the angel ship."

Konrad struggled not to react to her blatant lie. Was she trying to protect him, knowing he couldn't lie if asked? But how did

63

she know the *Blue Phantom* was near? Had she read his mind without his consent? Why couldn't he sense her mind intrusion? This woman was so irritating… but also very kind, despite her many flaws.

Zethar seemed to accept her claim. "In any case, you are caught now, this is the end of the line for you, little lady."

"My name is Valka, not little lady." So much bravado in her stance, head held high. "And if you think you have me pinned down, you are mistaken, Zethar. I will escape."

"Brave words, but I don't think so." Lord Zethar chuckled. "This is Azuran technology I adapted for just this kind of eventuality, and it is very effective in neutralizing all kinds of supernatural powers."

"Well, you never dealt with me and Sultan before." Still defiance in her voice.

The tiger hissed, as if offering moral support.

"Sultan, is it? Your tiger is a magnificent beast." Greed shone in Zethar's black eyes. "I used to have a lion as a bodyguard a while back… a magnificent champion from the arena. I can tell this tiger is worthy of a noble owner like me. I think I shall have him rewired to obey my commands. He will become my new bodyguard."

Konrad winced at the man's viciousness. He wished he could free Valka.

"No! Not Sultan." Valka's voice shook. Her face softened and she seemed close to tears. She obviously loved her tiger.

"Don't worry, you won't see it happen." Zethar's cruel grin was disturbing. "You will be too busy fighting for your life in the games... without your powers, of course."

Konrad was ready to explode inside but knew he must control himself. How could his captain ask him to deal kindly with such a despicable man? "Zethar, wait! Maybe, the delinquent should be made to pay for the warriors she stole instead."

Zethar turned an interested eye on Konrad. "That could work... but only if the price is paid in Azuran technology."

Konrad felt cornered. His suggestion had backfired. "My superiors will never approve getting involved in the settlement of a debt for someone who is not an angel."

Lord Zethar linked his hands behind his back and turned to Valka. "That's right, you are not an angel. So, where do your powers come from?"

Valka straightened and stared at the crime lord with a stubborn brow over her fascinating peridot green eyes. "None of your business, that's where. But I will never fight for your filthy games, and you can forget about stealing Sultan. Even without my powers, he and I will kill anyone who enters this cage."

"You are so naïve, little lady." Lord Zethar laughed.

Konrad didn't. He knew the crime lord had all kinds of stolen and illegal technology beside Azuran tech. Most certainly, he had the means to neutralize and control Valka... or any angel for that matter.

Chapter Five

From her cage in the filthy Menagerie, Valka found it difficult to ignore the stench and the moans of human and animal suffering.

She also struggled to slow her heartbeat as she watched the general and the crime lord walk away, and out of the Menagerie. The guards left as well. No one wished to stay in this stink hole any longer than they had to.

Why did her heart race every time she saw the angel? What was so special about him? The far memories of her long dead lover resurfaced again. Why?

Valka hoped he wouldn't get in trouble with his superiors because of her. Still, he should have pleaded her cause and freed her from Zethar. If not with angel tech, at least with gold. No miscreant ever refused a large amount of gold.

Valka needed to think. She had never faced captivity in her entire life, and the very thought frightened her. She absolutely refused to fight in the arena to entertain the rabble. But what if Zethar could make her fight? Could he? She hoped not.

She glanced at the warrior woman lying on the metallic floor plate. She checked her pulse... too feeble. The woman didn't have long to live. Valka must save her.

Sultan lay next to the wounded woman, head low, eyes sad. He emitted a kitten's soft whimper.

Valka patted the furry head. "Don't worry, Sweetheart. I'll get us out of here."

She hoped she could. All wasn't lost. Not yet. Even without her powers, Valka was still a highly trained warrior. Besides, all the Valkyries who had come before still lived in her, as long as she wore her armor. Could they help her?

She'd never asked for help before, but she must try. Although Valka had lost her powers, maybe their spirits could still hear her call.

Valka sat, cross-legged on the perforated steel plate forming the bottom of the cage and closed her eyes. Slowing her breathing, she emptied her mind. "Great Brunhilda, Goddess Freya, Father Odin, may your spirit and the spirit of all the Valkyries, send me a vision to guide me out of this predicament."

No answer, of course. Neither gods nor her sisters ever spoke to her in words.

"Sultan like Freya." The tiger intruded in her head, aware of the connection.

"Yes. The Goddess is here." Valka reveled in her loving embrace. How she missed Asgard... especially the love of her Asgardian sisters.

The image of a small electronic device attached to the widest top bar of the cage surged in Valka's mind. It emitted a strange magnetism. Could it be a power source, an antigravity device? A shield generator? Or did its vibration somehow neutralize her abilities? Or all of the above? She couldn't tell.

The vision ceased. Valka opened her eyes and stood up to look more closely at the top of her cage. A wider, solid steel bar, shiny, naked and unremarkable, ran along the center. Yet, the cage could float, so it must have an antigravity system somewhere, and a power source.

Since the bottom of the cage was perforated and showed nothing underneath, it could very well be up there. Her visions never lied... but she couldn't see any device attached to the top bars... unless, it had its own invisibility cloak. Very clever.

If there was a device, Valka could never reach it, the bar was way too high. But maybe Sultan could jump that high.

She squinted looking up. "Sultan, can you see a small box attached to the top bars?"

The tiger pivoted his round ears then glanced up. *"Sultan see no box."*

"Can you pretend there is a box in the middle of the wider top bar, and grab it with your claws?" She made her voice playful, as if talking to a child.

Sultan sprung to his feet and harrumphed, eyes round, ears straight up. *"Sultan play?"*

"Yes, Sweetheart. Play and knock down that imaginary box for me." Valka wished she had a laser pointer.

No matter. She removed her belt and captured the light of the closest sconce with the buckle's crystal inlay. Shards of light bounced off the flat steel bar, in the precise location where the vision showed her the invisible device.

Broken shards of light scintillated where Valka aimed. Sultan wriggled his rump then leapt toward the dancing lights, claws extended, emitting joyful sounds. He missed and landed.

"Try again! Catch that light!" Valka made the light shimmer in the right spot.

Sultan jumped and clawed at the bar, hanging from it, trying to get the light before coming down.

He landed, and something clattered to the metal floor of the cage.

Valka rushed in the direction of the sound on all fours. Feeling her way across the perforated floor plate, she hit an object the size of a fist and grabbed it. She still couldn't see it, but she had it. Now she must destroy it. Electronic devices were delicate by nature.

Holding the device in her left hand, she drew her dragon fang blade and pounded the object with the butt of the metal grip, as hard as she could, under Sultan's curious stare.

The hammering sound carried through the entire Menagerie, attracting glances from other prisoners. Valka must hurry, before the guards outside noticed the sound or saw it on their monitors.

On the fourth strike, the object became visible. A simple rectangular black box, just as the vision had showed her. She turned it in her hands, looking for a trigger, a switch. Seeing none, she struck it again, reducing the device to bits.

One bit in particular rolled in front of her, a blue glowing marble that may have been the power source of the device. How beautiful.

Sultan saw the marble and went to sniff it. *"Smell like angel."*

"Must be the famous Blue Crystal." Valka grabbed the marble and stored it inside her belt, which she cinched and buckled around her waist.

As she rose, she felt lighter. She could sense a different vibration in the cage. She had her powers back. Yay!

First, she rushed to the wounded warrior and placed one hand on her chest to infuse her with stabilizing light. The circumstances didn't allow time to ask permission from the woman to save her. Valka hated doing things out of order. They must get out before Zethar realized what happened.

Valka carried the woman and laid her across the tiger's back. "Ready, Sultan?"

The tiger straightened. *"Okay. Sultan ready."*

Valka vaulted on the beast. "You don't need to spread your wings. It should be a smooth landing."

"Go where?" The tiger sounded happy to leave.

Valka closed her eyes and visualized her destination with the image and shield codes borrowed from General Konrad Lagarde's mind. "To the *Blue Phantom!*"

* * *

Konrad followed Zethar inside the Pandemonium Command Center, wishing he could be back on the *Blue Phantom*. The close proximity of sin, cruelty, and debauchery affected his natural serenity. How could people live like this?

The crime lord glanced up at the screens on the clear Flexglaz wall surrounding the top of his office and froze. "Where is she?"

"Who?" Konrad glanced up.

Zethar slammed his fist on his desk. "The woman and her tiger are not in their cage anymore. Nor is the wounded Priory slave! How am I going to explain this to the Abbotts?"

"The slave thief vanished again?" Konrad stared at the Menagerie screen in surprise, trying to hide his pleasure at her escape. "I don't understand."

Zethar paced his office. "Not even an angel can escape that trap." He stopped and stared at Konrad. "You must have helped her somehow. How did you do it?"

"I didn't help her. I didn't do anything. How could I? I was with you all this time. In any case, angels cannot lie." Konrad was offended and mortified by the accusation. "Besides, why would I help her? She isn't one of us."

"If she's not an angel, then what is she?" The anger in Zethar's voice vibrated throughout the Command Center.

Konrad refused to betray Valka's nature. He wanted to protect her but could not lie. "I can't believe she escaped."

"Give me the means to find her, capture her, and hold her for good." The angry, hairless brow on the crime lord's smooth face left no doubt about what he would do to her if he found her again.

"Sorry, Zethar. As I said, this is not angel business." Konrad took a calming breath. "Angels do not get involved in catching criminals or in personal vendettas. We only fight evil entities when they threaten the balance of light and darkness in the universe."

"I remember a time when the *Blue Phantom* rescued the innocent attacked by pirates and Marauders." Sarcasm tinted Zethar's voice. "My kind of people..."

"We still do, but you are hardly innocent, Zethar." Konrad must distract the crime lord. How could the lovely woman possibly thwart angel tech? "Right now, we are busy recruiting the worthy to fight the next great battle."

"That's what you think is coming? Another battle with evil beings?" Zethar's eyes grew rounder and his face froze. "You think it's through the Priory, this time?"

"That's why we need your help. You have boots on the ground everywhere. You know what's happening in every sordid corner of this galaxy."

"I do." Zethar straightened and somehow, managed to look taller. "But why should I help you? You sure don't want to help me!"

"I must follow angel rules." Konrad was getting tired of dealing with this twisted man. "Will you help us or not? It's entirely up to you, of course."

"Not this time." Zethar locked his hands behind his back. "The tech you gave me last time obviously doesn't work as well as you claim. It is faulty. The thieving woman and her tiger escaped."

"I am sorry about that, but our tech works perfectly." Konrad bit his lips.

Zethar snorted like a steam engine. "Now I have to deal with the Abbotts and explain that loss. It's going to cost me lots of credits. I think you are trying to stiff me, General. I will not help you."

"I wish you would reconsider Zethar." Konrad must fulfill his mission. "Whatever evil is surging through the Priory can destroy your dominion in this quadrant as well."

Zethar reached under his desk and pulled out a very large phaser. Highly illegal and probably superefficient. The crime lord unlocked the safety then pointed the weapon at Konrad, slowly, deliberately.

Konrad suppressed a gasp. "You wouldn't want to start a war against the angels, Zethar." He made his voice menacing. "We can destroy this entire station in one strike."

"I know you can." Yet Zethar still aimed the weapon at Konrad. "Can a mega-phaser kill an angel? I'm curious."

Konrad hated the pinch of failure in his chest. "I see our negotiations have come to an end."

Deploying his wings, Konrad took a deep breath, visualized the command deck of the *Blue Phantom*, then dematerialized. One strike from this mega-phaser may not have killed him, but it would be painful, possibly crippling, and it would take a long time to heal.

Now, how could he explain his failure to his captain without lying or involving Valka? And why was he trying to protect her?

* * *

As she rematerialized with Sultan and the woman warrior inside the *Blue Phantom*, in a room that glowed like Blue Crystal, Valka expected the angels to question her intrusion. But the handsome beings in white robes who came to her smiled, and offered help instead. They directed her to Sickbay and took charge of the wounded woman warrior without question.

How naïve of them, but also generous. What if she had nefarious intent?

Inside Sickbay, where soft harmonies penetrated the body and the mind, Valka stared at the sleeping warrior on the floating medical bed. The woman was tall and strong. Even without weapons, she looked fierce in her armor made of woven fibers and metal threads... the perfect protection against blades.

Sultan sat at her bedside, as if guarding her, licking her face from time to time.

All around Sickbay, the bulkhead glowed blue, and the fragrance of cherry blossoms floated in the air. Just standing there made Valka feel good, as if the air itself had healing properties. It reminded her of Asgard.

A glowing angel of undetermined gender, with clear blue eyes and short blond hair, wearing a white robe with a caduceus on the sleeve, walked to her and bowed. "She will be fine and should awaken at any time."

"Thank you." Valka felt humbled by the love and dedication emanating from the angel. "The Guardian Angels of the Universe, as some call you, have a reputation of being just, but merciless against the wicked. Is that true?"

The angel bowed. "It is our purpose to smite evil."

Valka nodded, happy to be serving the greater good. "But I never suspected you could be so loving and generous with ordinary people."

The angel smiled. "There is nothing ordinary about you, Valka. And this woman is worth saving."

"I know." Valka's mission for many centuries had been to recognize and save or reward the worthy. And with the rise of the Priory, more warriors than ever needed her help.

"Your protegee is about to wake." The angel straightened, deployed white feathery wings, then dematerialized, leaving a trace of sweet fragrance in the air.

"Wow!" Although Valka often vanished the same way, it still amazed her when the angels did it with such panache... seamlessly, without the help of any device. Without her armor, Valka would only have her Zephyrian mind-reading ability.

Now, for the hard part. She must convince the warrior woman to fight for the angels. Valka had broken the rule by saving her without consent. In her escape, she had no time or opportunity to ask, and no other choice. But now, she must rectify her infraction.

The woman on the bed stirred and took a deep breath, then she opened dark brown eyes and glanced around. "What happened? Where am I?"

"You are safe, on the angel ship *Blue Phantom*, in Sickbay." Valka was glad to see the woman conscious. "My name is Valka. I rescued you from the slave market, and the angels here healed you."

"My name is Beatrix." The woman sat up. "Thank you."

"You are welcome." So much for not getting personal with her marks, or learning their names.

The woman turned and saw Sultan. Her hands went for a weapon at her belt and found none. "Where are my weapons?"

Valka smiled at the reaction. "Don't worry. Sultan will not harm you."

The tiger growled in ascent.

"And your weapons belt is in a compartment over there." Valka indicated the back bulkhead. Funny how true warriors felt naked without their arsenal.

The woman glanced at the bulkhead. "Okay."

"How do you feel?" Valka was breaking her rules... again. Why?

"I feel great." The woman stared at her left thigh and touched the place of the former wound. "Not even a scar?"

"The angels do wonderful work." Valka cleared her throat. "But their help comes at a price."

The woman narrowed her eyes at Valka. "What price?"

"You must agree to become an angel and fight in the next great battle against the forces of evil." Valka held her breath.

"And if I don't agree?" These suspicious narrowing eyes again.

Valka had never faced this situation. She always asked for a commitment before saving their lives. "I don't think you have much of a choice at this point, Beatrix. You are already on their ship, and I understand that prolonged exposure to its vibrations is enough to transform anyone into an angel over time."

A curious light shone in the woman's dark eyes. "Aren't you one of them?"

"No. I'm not an angel... although, we share many abilities, like being long-lived, and impervious to most weapons." Valka must stop divulging personal information.

The woman smiled. "Since my planet is now under Priory control, I'm a warrior without a cause. Yours seems worthy. I could see myself as a warrior angel."

"Great." Valka let out a sigh of relief. "So, you accept to fight with the angels in the great battle?"

"Why not? That's what I do best." The woman took a deep breath. "This is going to be fun."

"Fun?" Valka shook her head. "Welcome to the *Blue Phantom*."

Chapter Six

Konrad walked briskly along the luminous corridors of the *Blue Phantom* to rid himself of nervous energy. He'd failed in his mission to recruit Zethar as an ally. How humiliating. He wasn't cut out to be a diplomat.

As he spotted Valka and her tiger coming out of Sickbay, he halted, heart pounding. He couldn't believe it. "Does the captain know you came aboard?"

The tiger hissed at him.

"Of course." Valka closed the distance then stopped, facing him. "The healers informed her when I brought a wounded warrior onboard as a new recruit." Valka seemed to enjoy her small victory.

"And the captain didn't object?" Civilian angels had no regard for the rules.

"Not at all. I work for Azura. Remember?" She winked at him with these fascinating green eyes. "She granted me free access to the *Blue Phantom* at any time."

Unbelievable. "But how did you manage to come onboard?" The *Blue Phantom* was cloaked and shielded. "Only angels can materialize on this ship."

Valka scoffed. "I may not be an angel, General, but I can see whatever I wish in anyone's mind... even shield codes."

"You stole the codes and the location, as well as the configuration of this ship from my mind?" How dare she? Konrad felt the need to vent his righteous rage.

"Sultan see angel ship too," the tiger said in a strong mind voice, proving once again that he had many abilities.

Valka straightened her frame and gave Konrad an exaggerated salute. "Permission to come aboard, General."

"A little late to ask permission, isn't it?" Konrad shook his head in frustration. "Reading an angel's mind without his knowledge or consent is extremely rude." Why couldn't Konrad feel her intrusive presence in his head?

"Forgive me. I never thought of asking. I read your mind when we met on the slave market." She shrugged and scratched the tiger's head. "It was a good thing, since it allowed me to manifest inside your ship."

"How brazen of you." And how disturbing that he didn't feel it... and humbling to admit. Not to mention potentially dangerous to the security of the angel ship.

The tiger sat and stared at him with unsettling intensity. *"Sultan read mind too. Not like Angel Konrad."*

How upsetting for an angel not to be liked... even by an animal.

The lovely woman relaxed her stance and chuckled. "What's the point of reading people's minds if they know it's happening?

When I do it, no one ever realizes it. Not even angels."

"Evidently." Konrad fumed.

She seemed to enjoy his humiliation. "For me, it's child's play."

Konrad didn't know what to do with this information. Such beings as Valka could present a serious security threat, but the captain allowed it, and her word was law on the ship.

Valka's face turned serious. "But when I was in that cage, I couldn't read anyone. All my powers were gone. What kind of trap was that?"

"Sultan not like cage. Sultan scared." The tiger head-bumped Valka's arm.

She obliged the big cat with a head scratch. "You are safe now, Sweetheart."

Konrad suddenly wished he was the recipient of such loving attentions. He pushed away the intimate image in his head and cleared his throat from the choke of embarrassment. "That cage uses angel tech. We have similar neutralizing cells aboard the *Blue Phantom*, to damper the powers of rogue angels and evil entities."

"You have rogue angels? That's interesting..." She walked around him, slowly, eyes narrowed, observing him from all angles. "And how did Zethar acquire such restricted technology?"

Konrad took a deep breath. Since she could read his mind, there were no more secrets. "Well, a while back, Zethar's illegal tech helped us trap and banish the evil entity Nyxor, and destroy his minions. It saved the galaxy. In return, the angels gave him whatever he wanted."

"Wow! You willingly gave angel tech to a crime lord?" Valka's condemning stare matched the accusatory tone.

"I also do not approve, but it seemed like a fair trade at the time, given the alternative." Konrad wanted to say he would never have agreed to such a deal, but it would be a lie. He'd almost made a similar bargain with Zethar just an hour ago. "In any case, I wasn't aware of that transaction at the time. I wasn't on the *Blue Phantom*."

"Why not? Where were you?" Her body tensed, and the light in her striking green eyes intensified.

"I was on Azura, fighting a desperate battle for the angel planet." Images of angels with charred faces and broken wings falling from the sky and splatting in the burning jungle made him wince.

"I see..." Valka sounded sad, as if she understood... or was she reading his mind? "Who could possibly overcome Azura's planetary defenses? I thought they'd never been breached." Her peridot eyes studied him.

Konrad shouldn't divulge Azura's weaknesses, but he was powerless under her gaze. Besides, she could read whatever she wished in his mind. "The enemy generated some kind of anticrystal EMP that neutralized all the crystal on and inside the planet. Everything on Azura is powered by crystal, even the planetary shields, and all our weapons."

"So, what happened?" Her hand went to the hilt of her dragon fang blade, as if ready to fight for Azura.

"All our military AIs switched off. All our ships stalled. Mine crashed and burned. I was critically injured, but I survived. Most of my crew did not. We lost ninety percent of our Avenging Angels in that battle. We would have lost everyone, if not for the *Blue Phantom*. They neutralized the evil entity and managed to banish it from our universe."

"So, that's why Azura is recruiting warriors?" She nodded in understanding. "You lost your entire army?"

"Almost all of it." Konrad sighed. "Nyxor, the evil entity in question, swore to return in full force and kill us all. We must be ready."

"Will you be?" She narrowed her green eyes at him.

Konrad realized Valka was steering him into a different conversation and refused to let her manipulate him. "What I want to know is how you escaped from that cage."

Sultan harrumphed. *"Cage scary."*

"Sorry, General. A girl is entitled to have secrets." She winked at him then turned away.

"Not so fast. There are no secrets on the *Blue Phantom*." Konrad attempted to read her mind but met a mental wall. "Angels don't keep secrets."

"Maybe, that's your weakness, General." She scratched the purring tiger. "You tell the truth and you follow rules, but your enemy doesn't."

"We prefer to see our inability to lie as a strength, and our rules benefit and protect all angels." Konrad wished he could make her understand total honesty united the angels and made them stronger. "In any case, because of your little stunt, Zethar is refusing to help us against the Abbotts. He thinks we gave him faulty tech on purpose."

"But you didn't." She definitely enjoyed sparring with him.

"Of course, not. We always keep our word." Konrad sighed.

"Sorry for the inconvenience, but I hate being caged." Her smile said she wasn't sorry at all.

Konrad shook his head. "Now we have to find other ways to get the pulse of the galaxy, and risk many angelic lives on dangerous spying missions."

She looked him up and down. "I'm sure even you can understand I had to escape. I didn't have a choice."

"There is always a choice." Konrad wished he could arrest her for trespassing, but he couldn't go against captain's orders... or give her back to Zethar. He also suspected

Valka wouldn't go willingly, and they'd have to fight... a completely different wrestling scenario unfolded in his head. He pushed the intruding thoughts away from his mind.

"Like it or not, General. I do what is necessary to remain free to do my job." The fists on her hips confirmed her resolve.

Konrad struggled not to express his frustration. "Your methods are reckless and irresponsible. They are not compatible with angel rules and philosophy, therefore, they are unacceptable to us."

"Hey, don't tell me how to do my job. I'm on your side." The aggressive battle voice startled him.

Konrad tried to relax and calm himself. "And you have no remorse for the damage you caused."

"Not at all. They all deserved it." Her body relaxed. "Oh, I almost forgot." She pulled something small out of her belt. Something blue and glowing, like a luminous marble. "Here. You probably want that back. I assume it's yours. Sultan says it smells like angels."

"Sultan like angel smell..." The big tiger sounded happy but shook his big head. *"But not angel Konrad."*

"Be nice, Sweetheart." Valka handed Konrad the small crystal.

When Konrad reached for it, their hands touched, and it gave him a pleasurable thrill. Or maybe it was the vibration of the crystal... definitely Azuran.

"Thanks." He studied Valka closely, more intrigued than ever. "How did you get this?"

"It powered the device I destroyed to escape my cage." She hooked both thumbs in her belt in defiance. "Don't interrogate me like a criminal. I did nothing wrong. I was just doing my job when Zethar trapped me, like you are doing yours. And I gave back your crystal."

"And what is your job, exactly? Bounty hunter? Thief? Taking any high paying assignment, no matter the consequences?" Konrad couldn't stop his blaming tirade. "It seems you also killed a ruffian on Pandemonium. You do not seem to follow any rules."

"Valka not thief." The tiger balled up, ready to pounce on Konrad.

He took a step back. What was wrong with that cat?

Valka seemed amused. "You ask too many questions, General. But you are right. I do not follow anyone's rules... only my own."

"That's rather convenient." How could he like and dislike her at the same time? She seemed to enjoy pushing his buttons. "Or should I say your methods are opportunistic?"

"At least I have standards, General." She raised her head haughtily. "I don't get chummy with crime lords. I only rescue the warriors they enslave."

"Touché." Konrad had to admit she had him there.

"*Sultan fight?*" The tiger stared at the two of them in turn, poised, round ears pivoting, tail twitching.

"Stop, Sweetheart. We are not fighting." Valka patted the cat, who relaxed and rubbed against her.

The small crystal in his hand gave Konrad an idea. "You should come with us to Azura, to see for yourself how we train our new recruits."

Her gem-green gaze scanned deep into his soul. Was she reading him? How he wished he could hide his thoughts from her. But obviously he couldn't. What a predicament! And a serious security breach threatening all angels.

She held her gaze steady. "I know you are hoping to convert me to your angel philosophy if we spend more time together, General, but it won't work."

"Still, you have nothing better to do." Konrad felt guilty for trying to trick her, but he didn't want her to leave.

"I should go find more warriors to earn more credits." Valka's resolute tone surprised him. That greedy streak again.

"And what do you do with all your credits, other than buy genetically enhanced tigers?" Konrad couldn't help the sarcasm in his voice.

Sultan raised his round ears at the mention of tigers and froze. When Valka patted his head, the cat focused on his fastidious grooming.

"What I do with my credits is my private business, General, not yours." The lovely woman smiled, as if to soften the blow. "But I accept your invitation to Azura. I understand visitors are not allowed there, and I've always wondered what the legendary angel planet looked like."

"Wonderful." Konrad allowed himself a small smile. Her understanding wasn't quite accurate, but he wouldn't correct her. He would, however, make certain Valka remained in proximity of the Blue Crystal as long as possible. Prolonged exposure had extraordinary transformative effects, even on the most stubborn people.

The overhead alarm beeped. "General Konrad Lagarde, you are needed in the observation dome."

What now? Konrad straightened his tall frame. "Sorry, I have to go. Valka, Sultan, welcome aboard."

Konrad deployed his wings and dematerialized.

* * *

When Konrad rematerialized inside the observation dome, four officers and Captain Graziella formed a circle around the 3D message pad, showing the revolving stamp of Azura, the glowing blue planet. It meant

Azura's leaders would be listening on this transmission.

Captain Graziella the Merciful motioned for Konrad to join the circle. "Our latest intelligence transmitted a never before seen aspect of the Priory. During the rare meetings of their Supreme Council of the Six, the leaders actually removed their masks, and we can view the memory of that meeting from our angel spy."

"That should be interesting." To Konrad's knowledge, never had the top leaders of the Priory revealed their identity, not to the public, not even to their own members. "Is the angel providing this intel safe?"

"As safe as she can be in the heart of enemy territory." The captain's voice shook a little, indicating concern.

Konrad closed his mind to what could happen to an angel caught spying on that evil sect. Spying on the Priory was deemed a capital offense, and breaking the rules often carried deadly consequences.

On the 3D pad, the floating logo of Azura melted, replaced by the image of a dark cavern with high vaulted ceilings lost in shadows, and a reddish glow enveloping an oval stone table. Vapors wafted around the dim light of the sconces, and smoke made it difficult to see. A sinister chanting pervaded the space, and the red glow seemed to ebb and flow with the fluctuations of the chant.

It reminded Konrad of other dark caves with the same kind of evil vibes, several cycles ago, during his time in the GTA. He shivered with dread.

Six imposing figures entered from different directions and stood around the stone table. Their high headgear concealed their heads and faces. Long, silky robes– red not black– covered their bodies. The gold seals hanging on their chests scintillated, inlaid with many-facetted rubies, indicating the highest level of authority in the Priory. These were not simple Abbotts. They also seemed very tall and muscular under the robes. Definitely not monks, but genetically enhanced super-soldiers. Military leaders.

Konrad shuddered at the thought. This all seemed too familiar. Top military brass taking control of a religious sect... just like the GTA did, not that long ago.

As the six figures pulled off their headgear at the same time, Konrad held his breath. The cleanly shaved heads made it difficult to distinguish men from women, but it seemed to be three men and three women. Then, as the leaders sat, the angel transmitting the images focused on each face, one at a time.

The tedious study of one face after the other revealed nothing.

Captain Graziella sighed. "How disappointing. None of these are influential heads of planets or known organizations."

Konrad kept watching. "They are nobodies." Then he gasped and pointed at the only leader still standing, obviously the one in charge. "Except this one."

"Freeze the hologram." Captain Graziella gave Konrad a curious glance. "He doesn't look familiar. Do you know who he is?"

The shaved head on the hologram revolved, showing a laser burn on one side of the face and many nasty blade cuts and stabs. The kind of face parents would use to scare young children and keep them in line. But for Konrad, each of these scars had a story, and he remembered inflicting most of them.

The other four angels on deck exchanged questioning glances and comments, but all shook their heads.

Cold chills ran down Konrad's spine as he stared at the familiar face. "I used to know this man, a very long time ago, but I thought he was dead. He was an admiral in the GTA. He dreamed of ruling the galaxy. He conspired against other GTA leaders. He sent millions of soldiers to their slaughter to advance his career."

Konrad had to stop. Deep emotions too long held back threatened to overcome him. "This man was once my mentor and my commanding officer. His name in the GTA was Admiral Krow, but we called him Killer Krow."

"Resume holographic transmission!" Graziella's order stopped all comments.

"Nyxifer the Powerful is near." The former admiral spoke in a strong commanding voice.

The angels on deck gasped at the name.

Konrad winced at the painful memories he'd buried deep down. He'd had nightmares about it recently. Maybe this was the reason. Killer Krow was alive and had resumed his reign of terror.

In the hologram, Admiral Krow straightened. "We must prepare for the coming of our benefactor, the bringer of darkness and order. He promises unchallenged supremacy and extraordinary powers still unknown to our galaxy. Only in the shadow of his darkness can we reign supreme. Hallowed be the name."

Then Krow fisted his chest. "Hail Nyxifer!"

"Hail Nyxifer! Hail Nyxifer! Hail Nyxifer!" the five other leaders answered with the same gesture.

Dread ran through Konrad as the gesture awakened bitter memories. He'd saluted ambitious GTA officers the same way in his dark past. He knew the measure of their greed and cruelty.

The meeting went on divulging the positions of armies and targeted planets. The angel leaders and officers everywhere had now witnessed the entire meeting and the Azuran High Council was informed. When the hologram ended, leaving the space empty, Captain Graziella seemed perplexed.

"I was wrong, Captain." Konrad blurted, breaking the silence. "About using angels as spies. This courageous angel has proven extremely useful indeed. May she remain undiscovered and unscathed."

"We all keep her in our minds, in a protective embrace." The captain rubbed her chin. "General, how do you happen to know the identity of the Priory's secret leader?"

The other officers gathered around to listen.

"I would prefer to forget these memories." But Konrad's mind kept returning to his time in the GTA.

"Tell us. Maybe it will be therapeutic. Maybe we can help you heal." The captain's voice held compassion.

Konrad couldn't lie or keep secrets anyway. "In my young mind, rules didn't matter as much as right and wrong. Once, I broke the rule of secrecy by telling a close friend about my suspicions that Admiral Krow was leaking information to the enemy in a conspiracy to take over the GTA council."

Konrad sighed, but wanted to tell it all. "When the next battle ended in a fiasco, the admiral quickly rose to power with enemy help. Then he accused me and my friend of leaking vital information that cost us the battle. Upon the admiral's word alone, my friend and I were convicted of treason and condemned to death by public execution."

"No wonder you want to forget it. What happened next?" The captain kept a strong but friendly attitude.

"My friend was executed." Konrad tried to suppress the horrible image in his head. "But I escaped and faced Killer Krow man to man. I was weak from torture, and he almost killed me, but I left my mark on his body. Before we could finish the fight, we were attacked by angels. Explosions separated us. Krow was gravely wounded in the battle, and I assumed he died in the total destruction of the base, but he must have escaped, somehow."

"That is unfortunate." Graziella's face held no mercy.

"After the fall of the GTA, I volunteered to join the angels... because they could not lie and followed strict rules. That was several cycles ago." But the memory of deprivation, torture, and abuse in a GTA prison remained fresh in Konrad's mind.

The captain stood straight, hands behind her back. "What can you tell us about Admiral Krow, about the man?"

"So many things." Konrad paced, unable to find serenity. "He is ruthless, will do anything to win, has no ethics, no qualms about executing his own friends, and has an insatiable appetite for power."

"The perfect type to attract the interest of an evil entity." Captain Graziella sighed.

The handful of angels on deck nodded in empathy.

The message pad came alive with the revolving seal of Azura, the blue planet.

The captain swiped her console. "Azura, we receive you. What are your thoughts?"

A lovely lady in blue veils walked onto the holographic pad. "Nyxifer, the bringer of darkness, that's the entity Krow mentioned. What do we know about this Nyxifer?"

"Could it be another incarnation of Nyxor?" Konrad remembered recordings of the red entity, muscular, naked, with gleaming white horns, curled back like those of a ram.

"It's possible. Or it could be a relative." Captain Graziella rubbed her chin. "Nyx means darkness. Whether it's him or not, the two must be connected."

Konrad nodded. "The name similarity could simply indicate that they come from the same place... a place of darkness."

The holographic Azuran lady in blue veils rose in midair. "If that's the case, we may have a weapon against it. We analyzed the vibrations of Nyxor on the recordings we gathered when he first appeared a few cycles ago, and we discovered a frequency that should be effective against him, or anyone coming from that particular universe."

"You mean, we can kill that Nyxifer?" Konrad rejoiced at such good news.

The Azuran lady smiled. "We could not test the weapon, of course, but yes, we believe it can kill such an entity."

"That's wonderful news." The captain smiled.

The Great Lady nodded. "Since you are coming to Azura, we can also make modifications to the *Blue Phantom*'s weapons to include that particular frequency."

"Great." The captain straightened. "We shall head for Azura as soon as we collect our last batch of volunteer warriors."

"See you soon." The Great Lady nodded then vanished. The 3D pad stood empty again.

Captain Graziella swiped her console to access the overhead system. "Let's hurry to our last pick up." Then she turned to her officers. "You have your orders."

"Aye, aye, Captain," the four officers answered with a salute and turned away.

"I thought we didn't obey Azuran orders." Konrad couldn't help a hint of sarcasm.

The captain sighed. "Although we are not Azuran citizens, we are still angels, and in times of crisis, all angels must rally against evil."

"Of course." Konrad hoped the new Azuran weapon would work, but his military mind told him nothing was ever as easy as it seemed. "Admiral Krow is twisted and dangerous. He must not be allowed to gain unlimited power through evil means.”

“Too bad your mission with Zethar went sour.”

“Yes, that’s unfortunate.” So, the captain had seen his report. “I take all the blame.” Konrad hadn’t mentioned Valka’s role. “But since Zethar turned against us, he could pose a serious problem. He knows much about angel technology and defenses. If he ever chose to share this dangerous knowledge with the Priory, it could have devastating consequences.”

“Let’s hope he doesn’t.” The captain shook her short blond hair. “But I don’t think he likes the Abbotts.”

“Maybe not. But he does like credits.” Konrad worried about angel safety. Valkyries, rebel angels, greedy crime lords, and so many other unknowns could jeopardize the light in the fight against darkness.

Chapter Seven

As the *Blue Phantom* made its final descent on Azura, Valka stood at the edge of the ramp, Sultan heeling at her side. Around them, hundreds of volunteer warriors talked excitedly in hushed voices. The angel crew remained quiet, but their bright auras indicated they were excited, too.

"Welcome to Azura. Prepare to disembark," the captain's voice announced overhead, quieting the chatter. "Upon exiting, the new recruits will proceed to their training camp. As for the non-essential crew, they will be free from duty for dirtside R&R."

A few angels cheered. Some of them must have missed heavy gravity.

Valka's heart pounded. She didn't know what to expect. She'd heard so many rumors and legends about the angel planet... they couldn't all be true.

The captain on the com took a deep breath. "Superior officers and engineers will remain onboard as the ship proceeds to the shipyard. They will work in shifts, to oversee and facilitate the installation of the new weapons, as well as installing updates and making modifications."

The whine of the drives ceased. The angel ship must be hovering just above ground.

As Valka glanced back, scanning the volunteers for Beatrix and the young man she'd rescued recently, she didn't see them in the crowd. But she realized the diversity of the future angels. Some had blue skin, others green scales and webbed feet, some exhibited protruding fangs, and a few had more than four limbs. More arms to wield weapons could come handy in battle.

A whoosh of compressed air stopped her train of thought. The ramp lowered slowly and a gust of warm breeze blew in her face, loaded with hints of tropical blooms and sweet spices. It evoked bittersweet memories of Asgard in summer.

"Sultan like Azura." The big cat rubbed his head against her shoulder.

"So far, I like it, too, Sweetheart." She ruffled and kissed the tiger's head. "I guess, we'll find out what all the fuss is about."

When the ramp hit the grassy ground, Valka and Sultan walked down with the first wave. As they emerged into bright sunlight, Valka blinked then shaded her eyes. The ship had landed on a vast verdant square.

She could smell and taste the salt in the sea breeze. The ocean must be nearby.

Stepping on the grass, she felt a buzz of energy pervading everything, even the ground, as if the vegetation, the stone, and the dirt were conscious, even self-aware. This was not an ordinary planet. It was alive, breathing, reacting. Any Asgardian would recognize it as a sacred place.

Sultan leapt and pounced, then rolled in the grass like a kitten on catnip. *"Sultan like Azura."*

Valka laughed at his antics. "To think, lucky angels get to live here all their lives and take it for granted, thinking it will always be here... like I did on Asgard long ago."

To one side, the warriors lined-up then marched away in rows, following their angel guides toward small shuttles bound for their training camp. Valka recognized Beatrix, the tall warrior woman, at the head of her column. Some were born to lead.

Not Valka. She was a free spirit and hated giving orders as much as following them. Her love for freedom had cost her everything. Now she had no home, no family, not even friends to share her life. She was alone.

The tiger bumped her shoulder. *"Sultan friend."*

She leaned and bumped heads with the big cat. "Yes, Sweetheart. I have you. And you are more than a friend."

The ramp retracted behind them, then the angel ship lifted off, revealing the main temple in the background, with monumental stone columns and a frontal terrace at the top of wide stairs. The translucent roof dome glowed blue, like the temple on Byzantium, or the bulkhead of the *Blue Phantom*.

On the opposite side of the vast plaza, many other domes, all blue and glowing, formed some sort of town, with blooming gardens, ponds, and artistic fountains and waterfalls in between. The larger domes might be public buildings, while the smaller ones looked like private residences.

Valka looked for traces of the devastating battle two cycles ago but saw none. Life had quickly rebounded. A wall of wild vegetation encircled the entire community, as if the town builders had carved a perfect circle out of the jungle, several klicks wide.

As many angels walked the stone path toward the agglomeration of domes, Valka followed them.

"Come on, Sultan." She was curious to discover more.

The tiger started following her then stopped, sniffing the air. *"Sultan smell prey."*

"Prey? Really? You just ate two protein packs. You can't be hungry." Valka wondered what kind of prey that might be.

Sultan licked his lips. *"Prey fun to chase."*

"You were grown in a lab, Sweetheart. You never had to hunt for food." But maybe his hunting instincts were sharpened so he could use them in combat.

Then Sultan emitted a strange kitten mew and froze, like a statue, neck extended, round ears forward, staring straight ahead.

Valka followed his stare and gasped. There, thirty meters away on the path, two gigantic cats with silvery coats and long saber fangs, loped with nonchalance, sniffing the air and the ground. Valka didn't know such great beasts could exist on a populated planet, even less live alongside people. Well, angels were not exactly regular people.

The angels closest to the giant cats didn't seem to notice or mind them. Valka attempted mind contact with the cats and was rewarded by a welcome greeting.

"Whoa!" She chuckled. Of course, if the vegetation was alive, the animals would be highly conscious, self-aware, and telepathic. What an incredible place!

Sultan sniffed ahead and emitted a low growl.

Valka patted his head. "It's okay, Sweetheart. Don't be scared. The big cats are friendly. And you can talk to them."

"Sultan not scared." The tiger relaxed and stated calmly. *"I am Sultan."*

The giant cats sniffed in his direction. *"Welcome, tiny cat."*

Then the giant cats walked away from the path.

The tiger snorted then followed Valka's steps, head down. *"Sultan not tiny."*

"Right." Valka petted his muscular neck. "You are big and brave, and nothing scares you."

Sultan only grunted in reply.

* * *

103

Konrad left his residential dome as the red sun sank behind the rocky hill, into the ocean beyond the jungle. Familiar stars appeared in a cloudless sky. It seemed strange to wear long silk robes again, but the familiar glowing sword at his belt felt reassuring.

He couldn't help but admire how fast Azura was rebuilt. He still remembered the fire and smoke, and the devastation. No trace of it remained. The angels had worked diligently to rebuild. He shivered at the alternative.

The destruction of Azura would have left this galaxy defenseless against enslavement or extermination by the evil tyrant Nyxor... an abomination from another universe. Fortunately, the evil one lost in the end, thanks to the crew of the *Blue Phantom*, and was banished... but the evil one had promised to return.

Calls from large birds and mammals filled the night breeze, reminding him angels were guests on Azura. The planet brimmed with wildlife – most of it large predators.

The stars above shone brightly. The scent of flowers mixed with the sweet aroma of roasting fruits and vegetables. Tonight, under the stars, the Azurans celebrated the crew of the *Blue Phantom* for recruiting so many new warriors.

Not a whisp of vapor marred the starry sky. The clouds would come later, darkening the night, then opening the sky vanes, pouring waterfalls over plants and animals. Azura's climate was predictable and always punctual, with warm days and nightly downpours.

Konrad couldn't wait to see Valka at the celebration. He wanted to show her the wonders of Azura, the place he now considered his home away from the *Blue Phantom*. But the excursions outside the protected town would have to wait until morning, when it was safe.

His heart beat faster as he neared the main plaza, illuminated by floating bulbs. White awnings protected the tables offering plenty of food and drink. The sounds of flute, string instruments, light drums and tambourines reached his ears. There would be interesting conversations, and maybe some dancing... although Konrad, like any respectable soldier of his kind, did not dance. His strict military upbringing in the GTA didn't allow such frivolous public displays.

Valka was a warrior, too, but from a different culture. He wondered what she thought about dancing. When his mind's-eye imagined her seductively dancing for him with languorous moves, her fascinating green eyes like deep pools of luminous water, he shook his head to erase the vision and reconnect with reality. His shameful infatuation with the woman was causing inconvenient daydreaming.

He stepped into the vast square to the salutes of a few crew members and dismissed them with a nod and a smile. Tonight, there was no rank, no uniform. Everyone should be allowed to relax. Soldiers needed to unwind once in a while in order to perform at their best. Of course, his crew was not military, but old habits from his time in the military and his days in the legions of Avenging Angels, made it difficult to think like a civilian.

Konrad went straight for the elevated terrace in front of the temple, where the leaders of Azura usually gathered during these events. He climbed the many steps and quickly located the Great Lady of Azura, wearing diaphanous blue veils, and a glowing sword. She looked even more beautiful and ageless in person than in the recent hologram.

He walked toward her and bent a knee. "Great Lady. It is a pleasure to see you again in body and soul. Holographic communications just aren't the same."

The Great Lady smiled, and her blue aura widened and glowed. "General Konrad Lagarde. How goes your mission on the *Blue Phantom?*

Konrad bowed humbly. "I am learning to curb my tendencies for strict discipline, Great Lady. The *Blue Phantom* doesn't exactly follow our military rules."

The familiar laugh of Captain Graziella the Merciful reached his ears, then she emerged from a group of high-ranking councilors and approached Konrad and the Great Lady. Konrad straightened his back and saluted, military style.

"At ease, General." Captain Graziella the Merciful waved away his salute. She wore her ceremonial white uniform, not the off-duty robes. Then she turned to the Great Lady. "I can vouch for the general's hard work and dedication, My Lady. He is learning to deal with civilian angels... and with the rest of the universe."

"I see." The Great Lady chuckled. "General, being raised in an authoritarian military regime, and becoming an Avenging Angel didn't teach you much about the niceties of social interactions. This must be quite a different experience for someone like you."

"It is, My Lady." Konrad felt the heat of embarrassment reaching his ears. "But I will learn to cope. Captain Graziella has been very kind and patient with me."

"Thank you for your assessment of my performance, General." The captain smiled then reached for sweets on a passing tray. "If you don't mind, tonight we are off duty, and I want to sample every kind of sweet and dessert this feast has to offer."

The Great Lady nodded to Konrad. "General, you should mingle and enjoy yourself."

"Thank you, My Lady." Konrad bowed and turned around, not quite sure how to go about mingling.

As he climbed down the steps, he had a great view of the entire plaza. He scanned the guests and spotted a familiar silhouette, wearing blue armor in a crowd of white silk, with a great tiger in tow. Valka. He directed his steps toward her.

* * *

Valka strolled among the silk-clad angels in amazement. Their auras glowed with love, and they smiled at her. None of them feared Sultan. A few even petted the tiger on the head. Happy music floated on the warm breeze.

"Sultan like angels." The tiger purred, enjoying the loving vibes of the feast.

"I'm glad you do." Valka nodded her thanks as she accepted a pint of honey ale and a veggie wrap from a server's tray. She took a sip and found the ale deliciously sweet and bubbly. A bite into the flavorful veggies exploded with hints of exotic spices. A true pleasure for the taste buds.

In her lonely existence on the fringe of society, Valka never experienced this kind of hospitality... not since the lavish celebrations in the halls of Valhalla. Bounty hunters never got invited to fancy feasts. Their employers paid and dismissed them as quickly as possible, like a necessary evil. No

108

one of refined taste wanted to socialize with hunters and killers.

Besides, Sultan made ordinary people nervous. Since the destruction of her home planet, Valka had always lived alone, away from civilized society.

She dropped her empty pint on a passing tray and picked up a full one.

"Have you tried the sweets?" The deep male voice startled her. "Apparently, the captain is very fond of them."

Sultan at her side hissed a warning. *"Stay away, Angel Konrad."*

Valka took a calming breath to slow her heartbeat and turned around. He looked regal in white silk robes, and the sword at his sash glowed a brighter blue than before. She couldn't control her grin. "Well, well, well. General, I didn't know you attended such frivolous festivities."

He clicked his heels and bowed, hands behind his back. "I never used to attend these functions. Avenging Angels do not participate in such revelries. They celebrate only great victories against evil." His smile seemed forced. "And their celebrations include friendly sword contests, and feats of strength and agility."

"But you are not an Avenging Angel anymore, General. Still, you don't seem to enjoy this friendly atmosphere." She couldn't help the teasing tone. "Sultan likes it a lot."

The tiger brushed against her and frowned at the general. *"Go away, Angel Konrad."*

Hearing his first name in her mind, Valka had a slight frisson. She knew it was Konrad, but he was so formal, she would never dream of calling him that.

"Be nice, Sweetheart." She patted Sultan. "The general is a friend, and an angel."

The general reached a hand to pet Sultan but the tiger snipped at his hand. Not fast enough. Angels had lightning-fast reflexes.

"Did he get you?" Valka was embarrassed by Sultan's behavior. He'd never done that to a friend before.

The general chuckled. "No chance of that."

"I'm so sorry." Valka smiled in apology. "He's usually very friendly with angels."

Sultan stood at her side like a bodyguard. *"Sultan not sorry."*

Hands safely behind his back, the general looked over the crowd. "I'm not sure what we are celebrating. We are experiencing grave times, we know the enemy is near, and this energy would be better spent addressing the current threats to this universe."

"While your ship is being updated for the next few days, you are stuck here, General. There is nothing you can do tonight." Valka found it odd to be giving advice. "You should relax a little."

"Relax?" He flashed a quick smile, and for the first time his blue eyes softened. "That's what everyone tells me to do. I'm afraid it's not in my nature."

"Nonsense. Anyone can relax." Although, Valka understood being different and feeling like an outcast.

"I admire your ability to blend with non-warriors." His voice blended with the warm breeze from the jungle.

Should Valka confide in him? "A night like this reminds me of home... Asgard. We used to celebrate life at every occasion. Like Azura, it was a special place, imbued with divine energy."

"I'm sorry you lost your home." So much sincerity in his voice. Angels never lied. "I saw it in the Akashic records, it looked lovely."

"It was." She sighed. "Even after all this time, I still miss it."

Sultan rubbed against her and she indulged him with a scratch.

The general glanced away, toward a group of glowing domes. "Would you like to take a stroll away from all the noise?"

Something clicked in Valka's mind. She wanted to take the invitation, but she must keep her focus. This man was dangerous to her. Being alone with him on such a lovely night could lead to disaster. Even though the ale had no alcohol content, the very thought of intimacy with him made her dizzy.

"Sorry. I think I'm a little tired." She forced a smile to soften the lie. "I'd like to go home and sleep."

His blue gaze didn't waver. "Then let me accompany you to your temporary residence."

Valka couldn't refuse. It would be rude. "Thank you. It's very close." She turned to the tiger. "Sultan? Are you coming?"

The tiger shook his head. *"Sultan not tired."* The big cat looked away and switched his attention to a group of angels. *"Sultan stay outside."*

"Your call, Sweetheart." Now she would miss Sultan as a buffer.

The tiger snorted as he loped away with a fluid stride.

She now faced the handsome general alone. "Sorry about Sultan. He's a little possessive."

"A little?" The general chuckled and offered his arm.

She had to take it. It would be rude not to. The very contact of his firm muscles under the rough silk made her head reel. She struggled to remain standing.

"Are you all right?" The concern in his handsome face made things worse.

"I'm fine. Just a little tired." Her heart beat so hard, she struggled to keep it in her chest. She took a few slow breaths. "I guess, I do need some rest."

He covered her hand with his, keeping her steady as her legs softened. They walked side by side in silence, under the stars, on the stone path, along blossoming trees, fragrant bushes, rectangular water pools with floating lotus flowers, and lush vegetable gardens.

He glanced at her and smiled. "This place is what I think of as my home now. This is what I envision when I long for a place to recharge."

"I can understand that." Valka struggled to resist the pull of his strange power over her. She must be strong. Yielding to her attraction to him would mean her doom... and that of many others. She pointed to a small blue dome. "This is my temporary residence."

They stopped at the bottom of the three steps leading to a blue door. Two tall bushes of fiery flowers flanked the entrance.

She reluctantly let go of his arm. How she wished she could let herself love. But such irresponsible behavior could be disastrous. She cleared her voice. "I guess I'll see you again soon."

He bowed. "I'll pick you up in the morning to give you a tour of the warrior training facility... and other wonders Azura has to offer."

She couldn't possibly refuse. That was the reason she gave him for coming to Azura... visit the training facility... although her true motive may have been to remain close to him a little longer. Her involuntary smile probably said too much about how she felt about him. "Wonderful. I'll see you in the morning, then."

He took her hand and lightly kissed her fingers.

A frisson ran from her head to her toes, and she couldn't wipe the idiotic smile from her face.

As he straightened, their eyes met and her legs turned to mush. She thought she was going to melt.

"Until tomorrow, then. Sleep well, Valka." He turned around and walked away.

She watched his back retreat, hoping he would turn back, but he didn't. She could still hear him saying her name with this angelic baritone voice. She would probably hear it all night, but it could never be. She sighed with regret as she climbed the three steps.

The door lifted open and she entered the glowing dome.

The strange interior was both esthetically pleasant and utilitarian. No furniture, only crystalline surfaces, steps down to a sunken area with cushioned steps serving as benches. And very high ceilings... probably to accommodate deployed angel wings.

As for the amenities, the spa space bubbled and steamed with water from a hot spring flowing in a marble pool. Utilitarian and decadent, like nothing she'd ever seen before. Low countertops of Blue Crystalline material with only a vase of fresh flowers.

The space felt so strange and empty, yet soothing and relaxing.

Valka dropped her weapons belt, pale blue shorts and boots, then stepped barefoot down the stairs into the bubbling pool. Blossom fragrance rose from the warm waters.

Soon the water reached her body armor. The armor was so light, she didn't feel it on her skin. Its special weave, neither hard nor soft, molded her body perfectly and moved and breathed with her like a second skin. She always bathed with it. Her armor kept her safe, protected, and connected her with a higher power. Removing it would be unthinkable, as catastrophe might ensue.

While relaxing in the soothing waters, she could still hear Angel Konrad's baritone voice saying her name. And what she read in his mind sent warnings to her brain. Although the general may not know it yet, his desire for her was undeniable. So was Valka's attraction to him.

But she couldn't let it happen. Ever.

Chapter Eight

At sunrise, Konrad walked among the dripping parks and gardens, stepping around the puddles, inhaling the fresh scents of tropical blooms after the rain. His steps felt lighter than usual, in his white silk robes, loose pants, and soft boots. The glowing sword on his sash hummed with a reassuring presence.

He must be careful today not to betray his annoying infatuation with Valka. Such feelings would not only break the unspoken angel rule, they would be embarrassing, especially for someone who avoided romantic entanglements all his adult life. For a soldier like him, duty was paramount. Nothing should compromise the mission, or his commitment to the Formless One.

Konrad found Sultan lounging on the steps, across the threshold of Valka's dome, blocking the blue door, between two tall bushes of bright red tropical flowers.

The tiger growled at him. His dark stripes contrasted with the gold and white in his pelt, matching the sun's golden rays.

Konrad kept walking toward the door, aware of the cat's hostility. "Good morning, Sultan. Did you sleep outside?"

"Sultan protect." The tiger sounded proud of his bodyguard duties.

"There is no need to protect inside the compound. Only angels and friendly creatures live here." Konrad shook his head. "Didn't you get wet from the rain?"

The tiger yawned, baring sharp fangs and teeth like a warning, then he stretched his magnificent frame, spreading deadly claws. *"Sultan like rain."*

Rather unusual for a cat. "Then you will like it here. It rains every night. That's what keeps the jungle green, and the gardens in bloom."

"Rabbit eat green." The tiger inclined his head. *"Sultan chase blue rabbit."*

"Did you catch it?" The odds were slim.

"Sultan catch one time." The tiger hung his head. *"Blue rabbit run away."*

"Sorry." Konrad repressed a chuckle at Sultan's disappointment. "It's still impressive that you caught it once. These creatures are lightning fast."

"Rabbit very fast." So much disenchantment in Sultan's tone.

Konrad indicated the blue door with his chin. "Is Valka awake?"

"Awake long time." The tiger's patronizing tone in his head indicated Konrad should know that.

So, Valka kept warrior hours. Probably training before dawn. It seemed knocking might be intrusive. Besides, Sultan still blocked the door. "Can you tell her I'm here?"

"Valka know." Sultan cleared the three steps to the blue door.

It lifted open, and Valka stepped out, wearing full armor, boots, and an assortment of swords and knives. "I'm ready."

"Good morning." Konrad wondered if she slept with her weapons. "Azura is safe. You don't need all that arsenal here."

"These weapons are part of me. Bad enough that I had to ditch the blasters and phasers, since they don't work near crystal." She gazed at him and her wide peridot eyes twinkled. "I'm so used to wearing my blades, I would feel naked without them."

"Spoken like a true warrior." Konrad patted the hilt of his glowing sword. "This one never leaves me either."

She nodded, as if she understood. "Where do we go first?"

"You said you wanted to visit the training camp." That's how he'd convinced her to come to Azura.

The big cat rubbed his head against Valka's shoulder. *"Sultan come. Sultan protect."*

"Sure." Konrad would have to win over the big cat. He hoped Sultan's jealousy could be tamed. He wouldn't want to face that large feline in single combat.

"Where is the camp?" Valka glanced around.

Konrad pointed to a rocky mound. "Behind that mountain. You can't see it from here."

"How do we get there?" She shaded her eyes from the morning sun.

"*Sultan fly.*" The tiger deployed majestic wings.

Konrad shook his head, thinking better of it. "But you guys are not familiar with the shield and the fence."

She glanced around. "What shield? What fence? I see no fence."

"Well, there is a domed shield encircling the entire compound." Konrad pointed to the high wall of vegetation surrounding the small town. "See the slight shimmer? It's the fence. It protects us from the large predators residing in the jungle."

"Predators?" Valka frowned. "Like the huge Saber-cats I saw yesterday on arrival?"

Konrad chuckled. "The Saber-cats are domesticated and friendly, unless you antagonize them."

The tiger growled. *"Giant cat say Sultan tiny. Sultan big, not tiny."*

"Of course, you are a big cat." Konrad wanted to scratch the tiger's head but thought better of it. "It might be faster if I dematerialize the three of us, since I'm the only one familiar with the camp."

Valka had a slight hesitation.

Did she want to steal the memories of it from his mind instead? Like she did to transport to the *Blue Phantom*? Konrad hoped not. But the very thought of touching her brought up emotions he'd rather keep private.

She took a deep breath. "Truth is, I've never been transported before. I always transport myself and others."

The tiger's tail twitched. *"Sultan fly. Valka transport."*

"Well, you would have to trust me, of course." Konrad hoped she would let him. "It would be a new experience for you."

Konrad offered his hand to Valka. She hesitated again, then reluctantly took it.

As Konrad closed his hand on her fingers, he had a slight frisson but ignored it, then he placed his other hand on Sultan's head, hoping the cat would let him do it. The tiger flapped his wings. So did Konrad. It was better to rematerialize in midair, to avoid a rough landing.

"Here we go." Konrad visualized the training camp in his mind. Then he dematerialized the three of them, feeling tingles throughout his body.

They reemerged, hovering over the flat top of a cliff. "Now, we are outside the shield."

Konrad flapped his wings in the light breeze, holding Valka in midair with the power of his mind. Then he deposited her gently on the rocky top of the plateau.

Sultan flew down in a graceful arabesque then proceeded to groom himself, pretending to ignore them.

"Thank you for the lift. That was rather pleasant." Valka brushed herself as if she'd been through a cloud of dust. Then she glanced down the cliff. "That's quite a view from up here."

They overlooked a valley surrounded by high cliffs on all sides. On the flat ground below, a vast camp had been erected, with many training fields, landing pads, barracks, small flyers and transports. A complete military base.

Entire battalions of new recruits, evenly spaced in perfect lines forming perfect squares, practiced fencing. They moved in synchrony, punctuating each strike of their swords with energy-expanding battle cries.

Valka's face came alive with excitement. "Aren't you afraid of an attack from above? This camp could be a death trap."

Konrad chuckled. "Watch."

He picked up a stone and threw it in a high arc in the direction of the camp. When the rock hit the shield, it became visible, and the rock disintegrated.

"Oh, I see." She chuckled. "Never mind."

"We also have a planetary shield." Konrad felt in his element. "It disables electronics and all conventional technologies... so non-angel ships fall from the sky."

"I see..." She stared at the blue sky.

"And when threatened, angels can always vanish."

She nodded. "I can do that, too."

"Look over there." Konrad pointed to another area, beyond the many barracks, where other recruits practiced with bow and arrow on hundreds of perfectly aligned targets. All around the camp, the shield now shimmered in the morning sun, just like around the town.

Konrad wanted to explain for Valka the mysteries of Azura. "What they are learning, besides the fighting moves and the skills, is how to focus on the Blue Crystal inside the planet, and use its energy to strengthen their strikes."

Valka nodded. "I understand. Most people only use muscles to fight, but true warriors charge their attacks with the life energy pervading the universe." She sounded proud of her knowledge. "I do it all the time."

The tiger interrupted his grooming. *"Azura make Sultan strong."*

"Exactly." Konrad smiled. "In time, these recruits won't need the sword or the arrows to focus Azura's energy. They will learn to channel it and use that energy as a weapon."

Valka narrowed her green eyes at him. "What happens when they are no longer on Azura?"

"Angels are never far from Blue Crystal." How he enjoyed being here with her. "Large chunks of it power our spaceships, space stations, and our outreach temples... You've seen one, floating high in the temple dome on Byzantium."

"I have." She squinted at the recruits below. "Is it true, all these warriors will become angels... with the long list of abilities that go with angelhood?"

"In time, yes." Konrad hoped Valka would remain on Azura long enough to become one. She would make such a wonderful angel. "And here, because the planet core is made of Blue Crystal, it happens even faster than on Byzantium, or on the *Blue Phantom*."

Her perfect eyebrows rose. "How long does it take?"

"Depends on the individual. Usually, weeks, sometimes days, sometimes months." Konrad hoped it wouldn't scare her into leaving. "Azura's lifeforce gives every living thing incredible energy, longevity, and extraordinary powers."

"I felt that energy as soon as we landed yesterday." She seemed in awe. "This is a very special place."

"Yes, it is." He was glad she could sense and recognize it.

"Sultan see blue rabbit. Sultan hunt." The tiger took off like a crazy kitten chasing a furry toy.

"Don't go too far, Sweetheart." Valka dismissed the tiger with a wave of the hand. Then she turned to Konrad. "I noticed everyone wears that same white fabric."

Konrad glanced at his robes. "It's raw silk. Very comfortable."

"Natural silk? From silk worms? Don't you have to kill the worms for that?" Was there a hint of teasing in her voice? "I thought angels did not kill innocent creatures."

"We do not." He snorted. "Unlike you on Pandemonium, throwing knives at thieves and jailors."

"They were all guilty of crimes, not innocent." Her voice rose stronger. "I would never harm innocent people or animals."

"That's good to hear." He meant it. "In any case, on Azura we do not kill the silkworms." Konrad was proud of the angels' way of life. "We grow their favorite bushes and allow them to mature and transform, then we collect the abandoned cocoons."

As he strolled along the cliff, she followed him. "The cocoons must be seriously damaged, no longer usable."

"True." He matched her pace. "That's why we reconnect the broken threads with crystal technology. The heavily repaired threads are the reason the weave looks thick and rather uneven. But the thickness makes the silk even more comfortable in cold space or in any climate."

"Good." Valka scanned the horizon then she glanced at Konrad's glowing sword. "Wow! Is your blade made of crystal?"

"Not exactly." Konrad drew his razor-sharp blade and held it to the light. It shone blue in the morning sun. "Azuran metal is stronger than crystal. Like everything else on Azura, it contains microscopic amounts of crystal melted within, and so, the blade glows, and it can be used to focus energy and strike. On Azura, it glows brighter because it resonates with the crystal at the planet's core."

"The planet has a solid core?" She had a cute frown. "Space rocks with no hot core don't usually support life."

Konrad chuckled, delighted at her interest in his favorite planet. "The surface crystal may seem hard, but at Azura's core, it is hot and liquid, and laced with molten metals."

"But how can crystal possibly transform people into angels?" So much curiosity in her voice. "Where does the magic come from?"

"It's not magic." Konrad shook his head at the common misconception. "It's a mixture of science and divinity."

Her eyes narrowed on him. "What divinity?"

"The Blue Crystal is a vessel that resonates with the divine frequency. It allows us to communicate directly with the Formless One. Through it, the Formless One makes us angels, and in return, the angels do the will of the Formless One, to preserve the balance of good and evil in this universe."

"Just like that?" She narrowed her green eyes at him. "And you never questioned that will?"

"Never." It would be unthinkable for an angel. Although, Konrad had never questioned the GTA either... until they crossed the line and showed their evil colors.

"Did it ever occur to you that this Formless One could be manipulating you for some hidden purpose?" Her tone of voice carried suspicion. "Why do you trust it?"

"We just do. The alternative would be too horrible." Konrad had no doubt. "For millions of cycles, the Formless One never lied, never failed, and always protected us."

"Except when Azura was almost destroyed, a few cycles ago." She crossed her arms as if daring him. "You said a great number of angels died in that battle."

"Yes." Konrad remembered the tragedy vividly. "Azura came close to total destruction, but it survived." He sighed. "And I hope the evil threatening us now will not succeed either."

Her green gaze swept the training camp below. "That's not very reassuring."

"No." He followed her gaze down the cliff. "But we do not hide from the truth, and we do not lie to each other. The warrior angels training today will face terrible odds. They know it. They chose to fight on the side of good."

"And they will be rewarded, in this life or the next." Valka's voice rang with absolute certainty.

"By the way, you never told me how you acquired your abilities." Konrad must find out if it constituted a threat for his kind, if evil could use it against Azura. Especially since she could read angels minds unchecked.

"My gifts were given to me as a maiden, by Odin, and his power came from Asgard." So much reverence in her voice.

Konrad nodded. "But Odin is long dead, and Asgard was pulverized, reduced to star dust."

"Yet, the powers of Valkyrie which Odin bestowed upon me survived after Ragnarök." The finality in her tone indicated that's all she would divulge.

"So, you trust that power implicitly, just like I trust the Formless One." Konrad rejoiced at his small victory. He had her there.

She chuckled. "Touché."

"I noticed your armor. I've never seen anything like it." Konrad wanted to touch it but would never dare. "What is it made of? What gives it the pale blue color?"

She seemed surprised and hesitated. "I don't exactly know. It was also a gift from Odin. Although it's light and flexible like a garment, it can stop blades, bullets, and energy bolts, even phasers and blasters."

"That's impressive." Konrad suspected there was a lot more she didn't tell him, but he wouldn't push it. According to the Akashic Records, Odin and Asgard had a positive influence throughout the universe. "Thank you for answering my questions."

"I guess, trust goes both ways." Her smile brightened her green gaze.

Konrad rejoiced. "Despite our vastly different cultures of origin, you and I have the same fundamental beliefs of good and evil, duty and sacrifice, and rewards in the afterlife for the worthy."

She shook her head and her flaxen braids shone in the morning sun. "Yet, you insist on calling me a greedy mercenary, with no loyalty and no honor. I resent that."

"Please accept my deepest apologies. I didn't know you at the time." Now that he had her talking, Konrad didn't want to antagonize her. Although he still wondered what she did with all the credits she must have collected in her long career as a bounty hunter. "I've come to trust you."

"Good." Her clear peridot eyes stared straight into his soul. "I remember seeing AI warriors on the *Blue Phantom* and on Byzantium. Isn't most of your military force made of AIs?"

"Not anymore. The biologic crew of the *Blue Phantom* is made of civilian angels with limited military training." Something Konrad planned to rectify. "Our self-imposed mission is one of peace and rescue of the innocents. Whenever we find ourselves facing a hostile armed force, our AIs fight for us."

"Do angels get in trouble?" She sounded amused. "Does it happen often?"

"Often enough to keep a contingent of AIs onboard." Konrad pointed to the sky. "In any case, Azura still keeps a strong AI army on the big ships orbiting the planet."

"So, why train so many new recruits?" Her chin indicated the trainees in the camp below.

"In the last great battle, we realized how vulnerable AI could be." Konrad fought the painful memories threatening to overcome him. He'd lost so many brothers and sisters in that battle.

"What happened?" Would her curiosity ever stop?

He took a deep breath. "A weird EMP struck at the planet's crystal core and disabled our ships, our shields, our weapons, and our entire AI army in one strike."

Valka's green eyes rounded in surprise. "No wonder you took a beating."

"It was horrible." Konrad still had nightmares about it. "That's why now, we make sure we also have a strong legion of live Avenging Angels handy with not only blasters, but also sword and bow to back it up if the technology fails. Hence, the new volunteers."

"That's wise." She glanced at the camp down below. "It shouldn't take long to beat these new recruits into shape. Most of them are already warriors."

"They'll be ready in a few weeks. By the time they get their wings and learn to fly, their training will be complete." Konrad hoped it would be enough to repel whatever evil was festering inside the Priory.

She shaded her eyes from the rising sun. "I assume you have more stops on that tour of Azura. What's next?"

"You were curious about the crystal. How about a closer look?" Konrad looked forward to this stop.

"Okay. But it seems we lost Sultan." She shaded her eyes to look around. "Should I call him back?"

"Let him run and chase blue rabbits." Konrad couldn't refrain a smile. He never wanted this day to end. He so enjoyed her company, especially without the possessive cat's interference.

Chapter Nine

Valka scanned the rocky slope where Konrad had deposited her, then cast him a sidelong glance. Yes, she called him Konrad now, but only in her mind. She would never dare call him by that name aloud. He was so strict and controlled about rules and etiquette, he would certainly disapprove.

He shaded his eyes against the sun. "I like this view."

In the valley below, nestled in shadows, Valka could see the perfect circle of the Azuran town with its glowing blue domes and tropical gardens, surrounded by a dark green forest. The air smelled fresh, but the rock under her boots was black, as if charred by intense fire in the recent past... or blasted by the heat of space cannons.

She could feel the strong vibration of the planet rising from the ground. So much life force. She couldn't help but think of long-ago joyful times on Asgard. It, too, had crystal at its core. Could she be happy here? "Where is that famous crystal?"

"It's everywhere." Konrad's blue eyes sparkled, and he flashed a mysterious smile. "This hill is full of it, right under our feet, inside a cave."

"A cave?" Valka wasn't prepared for spelunking. "I didn't bring a rope or a light."

"We won't need any of that." He motioned for her to follow him. "This way."

She walked behind Konrad at a good clip, down a narrow trail between black boulders, into a wide fissure. As they climbed down into the shadowy crevice, the side slits of his robe opened, revealing white silk pants tucked into soft boots. She noticed his powerful stride, the strong thigh muscles stretching the fabric, and the width of his square shoulders. His short black hair smelled like the woods after the rain.

She found herself daydreaming, longing for his affection. "How far is it?"

"Almost there." He leapt down a few steps, then raised both hands to help her down.

Valka never accepted help... from anyone. She didn't trust anyone. But she didn't want to hurt his feelings. So, she smiled her assent.

She let him grab her waist for the last steep drop, enjoying the guilty pleasure of his contact... as if his body vibrated with the energy of the planet, and maybe hers did, too. The feel of his hands was so familiar. How strange that she trusted him.

He held her waist longer than necessary and smiled as he released her. "Follow me."

He turned around and disappeared into a narrow opening between the rocks. She followed him through a dark passage, just wide enough for one person at a time.

"We should have brought a... light." Her last word faded as she emerged into a bright blue glow bathing an immense cave.

Crystal, all around. Giant octagonal pylons of luminous blue, spiking the space in every direction above her head, like walking inside an overgrown geode the size of a hill. The smooth crystal floor, looked as if it had been melted flat on purpose, so visitors could safely walk on the glassy surface.

The crystalline musical harmonies floating in the air reminded Valka of the temple on Byzantium, as if a soft breeze played chimes on the pristine crystal shafts, and made them ring and tremble, although they remained perfectly still.

Konrad's sword glowed from the inside as he stood, immobile, hands together, head down and eyes closed, in deep meditation. Was he communing with the spirit of the crystal? The Formless One?

Valka quieted her mind to savor the feeling of pure awe. The cave resonated through her as well. Tears flowed unbidden. She understood why Konrad called this place home. She fiercely missed Asgard, but Azura was just as beautiful, magical, and sacred. Never in all her travels had she experienced such an affinity with a planet since she'd lost hers. Maybe this could be her new home, too.

Konrad laid a gentle hand on her shoulder. "It's impossible to ignore the power of the crystal when you are surrounded by it."

She glanced up at his face and stepped back. "By Thor's hammer, your throat is blazing like blue fire!"

He chuckled. "Yes. It's my crystal synching with the motherlode... like my sword."

"You have crystal inside your body?" That was a new trick.

"Yes. Avenging Angels who go on prolonged missions off planet are implanted with a crystal core..." He leaned against a slanted blue pillar. "The implant insures we don't lose our abilities while away from our base for months at a time."

"Like a personal energy core." She took a breath to digest the information. It wasn't so farfetched. Scientists had been mixing technology and biology for thousands of cycles.

"In the past, angels carried a crystal pendant on long missions, but these pendants were sometimes stolen." He grimaced as if recalling something painful.

"Who would dare steal such things and why?" It seemed futile.

"Some like to collect and trade angel artifacts. Others, who know about angel technology are eager to use crystal as a power source for their own tech." He sighed. "A ship powered by a crystal the size of a fist can run for a thousand cycles."

"Impressive... But I thought Blue Crystal disabled traditional electronics." It certainly deactivated her blasters and phasers.

"It does, but if you know how, some tech can be adapted to work with a crystal core... like we modified the ships that crashed on Azura to build our own fleet." He sounded proud.

"I see..." She tried not to stare at his glowing throat.

He gently touched the luminous spot at the base of his neck. "This is safer... although, for a short time, when a power-hungry leader learned of this, he had several angels slaughtered for their crystal."

"Wow!" Valka wondered how a simple human could possibly kill an angel... or a Valkyrie for that matter. Her mind wandered to the carnage of Ragnarök and the slaughter of her Valkyrie sisters... but humans didn't cause that catastrophe. Powerful gods did.

"These implants are not public knowledge." Konrad cleared his voice. "I would ask you to keep this to yourself."

"Of course." It seemed for people who couldn't lie, angels kept many secrets.

"As a matter of fact, maybe you should carry a crystal pendant." He sounded dead serious.

"Me? Why would I need crystal?" Valka had her own power source in her armor, and Asgardian crystal on her belt buckle. But how could she refuse such a rare privilege? It would be an insult.

"You never know when it might come handy." His blue eyes peered into her soul.

"Blue Crystal protects the angels. It can protect you, too, since you work for us."

"I don't need protection. I'm not afraid of anything." Did he hope the crystal would make her an angel? It wouldn't work. The source of her power was just as strong as his, and maybe stronger.

"Watch this." Konrad turned to the oblique crystal shaft behind him and reached to touch it... or rather caress it lovingly.

How odd. And it made her yearn for his caress...

The crystal beam now hummed at a deeper frequency, and a glowing bubble detached itself from the shaft and levitated to dissolve into a puddle in his palm. Then he covered it with his other hand, closed his eyes, and luminous rays escaped between his fingers.

After a few moments, he opened his eyes and removed his top hand. "Here it is."

"Wow!" She stared at the glowing object, a large pendant the size of his palm, flat and round, and on its surface the raised design of a perfect Valknut, with the three interlocked triangles or pyramids... identical to the white crystal design on her belt buckle.

How thoughtful to make it so personal. She wondered how much he liked her but was afraid to find out.

He pulled a silk cord out of an inside breast pocket and threaded it through the small hole at the top.

"You always carry silk cords?" Did he plan this all along? Should she feel flattered? Or angry about his manipulation? She wasn't sure how to react. This place seemed to mellow her aggressive tendencies... or was it him? She refused to change her very nature for a man... even an angel.

Then he offered her the pendant. "Just for you."

She couldn't help but take the glowing stone with reverence. "Thank you."

"You are very special. You deserve it." His eyes shone with so much intensity.

Any remaining doubts about his motives dissolved. Valka caressed the lovely pendant, so smooth and warm to the touch. "How did you do that?"

"I'm an angel." He smiled with so much trust in his honest face. "I can do many things."

"So, maybe you can help me put it on." She handed him both ends of the silk cord then turned around and held up her loose braids.

"With pleasure." His voice felt like a caress.

The light touch of his fingers and his breath on the back of her neck gave her delicious sensations. Even if they could never be together as a couple, she would savor every moment of closeness she could steal from him.

But she could never allow herself to succumb to his charms.

* * *

Konrad blinked in the bright sunshine as they emerged from the cave and climbed back to the slopes of the rocky hill overlooking the town. He was glad Valka accepted the pendant. It looked magnificent on her, and it matched her armor.... If not her green eyes. But if she kept wearing it, she would become an angel, and her eyes, too, might change color.

He'd also charged the pendant with his own energy, keeping both their crystals synched together, no matter the distance between them. If Valka ever were in grave danger, he would feel it, and the jewel would act as a beacon so he could go rescue her. Would she have declined the gift if she knew it also was a homing device? He didn't want to take that chance.

Valka shaded her eyes, scanning the town below through the shimmering shield. "What's happening over there?"

Konrad followed her gaze. About a hundred angels had formed a wide circle and hummed in unison. "They are raising a new dome."

"What do you mean?" She frowned. "They seem to be meditating."

"They are." Konrad so enjoyed her insatiable curiosity. "They do it the same way I shaped your crystal pendant. They focus on the minerals deep in the ground and bind their minds together to bring them to the surface and shape them into a residential dome. Because the ground is saturated with crystal, the domes are translucent, blue, and glowing."

"Wow!" Her green eyes widened. "How long does it take?"

He was glad she took an interest in his favorite place. "Less than a day, if they have enough angels, because it takes the power of many minds sustained over several hours, and it can be exhausting."

"I had no idea." She glanced up at the sky and the wind lifted her flaxen braids. "I can smell salt in the breeze. Is there an ocean nearby?"

"Yes. You are very perceptive. You can't see it because it's on the other side of the hill." Konrad deployed his wings and opened his arms, hoping she would accept the invitation. "In Sultan's absence, may I give you a ride? Flying offers a better view."

She considered him, head bent to the side, with a half-smile. "I would be delighted."

It almost sounded too easy, but Konrad was glad she was warming up to Azura, and to him. He wished this day would never end. He hoped he could save her from an eternity of greed and lawlessness. He hoped so much more... but it would be selfish to express it.

She stepped close. "For your information, I read your mind, and I do not need saving."

"Right." He felt mortified for letting his mind wander into selfish territory. "And reading an angel's minds uninvited is considered rude on Azura... unless it's an emergency."

She scoffed. "I don't abide by your rules."

"Right." He seized her waist, enjoying the sweet fragrance of her loosely bound braids. Her strong grip on his arm felt heavenly.

He flapped his wings and firmed his arm around her. "I've got you."

Konrad took off and soared straight up, then leveled and flew lazily, high above the jungle. The warm breeze carried the heavy scents of tropical blooms. As he banked in the direction of the ocean, swaths of lush vegetation alternated with shallow streams and bands of white sand. In the distance, the sun warmed the beach and made the cresting waves glitter like strings of diamond.

He heard and felt her gasp of surprise. "It's beautiful."

How he hoped Azura would work its charm on her. It would be so wonderful to have the same favorite planet.

Soon, he deposited her gently on the wet sand, at the edge of the ebbing waves. Large birds flew high above, calling to each other.

"I remember beaches like this on Asgard, with children playing in the sand." She frowned, shading her eyes from the sun as she scanned the length of the beach.

"Where are the children? I haven't seen a single one since I arrived."

Konrad sighed. He dreaded telling her. "It's because there aren't any on Azura."

"Really?" She blinked against the sun. "Why not?"

Konrad bit his lips. "As it happens, the crystal that blesses us with so many abilities, also prevents us from having children... as long as we are exposed to it."

"Oh?" She seemed surprised. "Why do you think that is?"

"The angels serving the Formless One are mostly warriors like the Avenging Angels, or monks, not parent material." Konrad hoped she would understand.

"I can see that." She stared in the distance over the dark blue waters.

"Children would distract us from the most important mission of all... keeping the universe in balance between the light and the darkness, and safe from any evil threatening that harmony by taking control." Konrad took his mission very seriously.

"That makes sense. Besides, children could also be taken as hostages in an attempt to corrupt angels." She was thinking like a warrior. "And your civilian angels seem to live like the monks, meditating or working all day."

For some reason, Konrad felt relieved. "So, you get it."

"Of course, I do. Duty first." Valka made a wry face. "Well, Valkyries can't have children either… When we pledge to defend the realm and receive our gifts from Odin, we become sterile, probably for similar reasons."

Konrad couldn't help a grin. "On Azura, it's a good thing. Children wouldn't be safe here. We often deal with evil forces. And there are so many dangers in the surrounding jungle. Children would be easy prey to the many predators."

He motioned to the ocean with his chin. "Lots of sharks and giant crabs in there, too."

"Well, this planet is definitely teaming with life." She didn't sound disappointed at all. "So, if no children are ever born here, the only way to repopulate Azura is to bring more volunteers."

"Exactly." He smiled. "But because of our longevity, it doesn't need to be repopulated every generation… only when we suffer great losses… like we did in the great battle two cycles ago."

"I see…" Valka frowned then turned away from him and shaded her eyes. "Sultan, is that you?"

"*Sultan like fishies.*" The big cat raced toward them, splashing in the shallow waves, frolicking and leaping to pounce on quick silvery prey.

Konrad laughed at the cat's antics. The sound startled him. He hadn't laughed in a long time.

Valka stared at him, eyes wide in surprise. "I don't remember you ever laughing out loud since I met you. Azura must be good for you."

"I guess it is." She understood him so well... maybe because she could read his mind. Although he suspected she didn't pry too deep. Still. He wondered how much she knew about him. He'd made grave mistakes in the past, and some of his memories still brought him shame.

A horn sounded in the distance.

She turned to look in the direction of the town. "What is it?"

"Lunch time. Are you hungry?"

"I'm starving." She petted the tiger. "How about you, Sweetheart?"

The tiger danced around her, begging for more pets. *"Sultan not hungry. Sultan eat fishies."*

Valka scoffed then turned to Konrad with an apologetic smile. "I'm so sorry. I know you do not approve of killing for food."

"Angel rules do not apply to our animal friends." Konrad extended a hand to pat the big cat

The tiger growled a warning.

Konrad thought better of it and removed his hand.

"I'm sorry. He usually likes angels." Valka patted the cat instead. "It's okay, Sultan. You can stay here if you want."

Konrad would have to win that cat. "But Sultan must be back to the town before dark. Someone will have to transport him through the fence before nightfall. The jungle is not safe at night, even for a tiger."

"No problem." She scratched the furry chin. "Don't wander too far, Sweetheart, and answer when I call you in your head, okay?"

"Sultan answer." The tiger ran back to splash in the waves.

Konrad watched him from a distance, wondering if the big cat would ever accept him as a friend.

* * *

Back in the town of glowing blue domes where Konrad had rematerialized them, Valka felt light and happy as she followed him to the communal courtyard, where lunch was being served. She could smell the sweet and hot spices from the vegetables on the grill, and it made her mouth water.

They sat on wooden benches on each side of very long tables. Valka enjoyed the grilled fruit and vegetables presented on long trays made of interwoven leaves. Fragrant red tea made from tropical blossoms was served in blue glasses. The surprisingly delicious desserts dripped with spiced honey.

All the angels dressed alike, in white silk, and they ate in silence, like ancient monks. Unlike on Asgard, where banquets were noisy, lavish with meat and mead, and sometimes decadent.

Valka was glad Konrad agreed to keep her company and answer her questions. She so enjoyed talking to him. "I didn't see any fields nearby. Where is the food coming from?"

He held up a piece of red fruit. "Some fruit, like this one, is harvested in the jungle, but we also have hydroponic domes where we cultivate everything we need."

"Like on the *Blue Phantom*." It made sense. "How long is the *Blue Phantom* going to be immobilized?"

Konrad licked juice from his fingers. "Probably seven to ten days. The weapons updates are significant."

An angel materialized next to Konrad. "General, there is a group of volunteers ready to be picked up at our temple on Carina Prime."

Konrad nodded. "Prepare a small transport and I'll pick them up in a few hours."

Valka wasn't ready to let him go. "I could go with you, keep you company."

"No. It's better if you stay here." He returned to his brisk manners when other angels were around. "Besides, Sultan needs you."

Valka didn't believe Sultan needed her that much, but she didn't want to argue. "Okay."

Konrad caressed her hand. "I'll be back later tonight and we can continue our tour tomorrow."

Valka enjoyed his touch, but wasn't fooled by his subtle manipulation. She didn't like being left behind, but she didn't want to make a scene. Why didn't he want her to go with him?

Konrad smiled. "You can come with me to the shipyard after lunch and I'll give you a tour before I leave."

"All right." Valka hoped she could change his mind. For some reason, she didn't want him to go off world without her.

Chapter Ten

By the time Valka and Konrad flew into view of the shipyard, the afternoon sun had warmed the air. She enjoyed hanging on to Konrad's waist in a tight embrace, as the flapping of his feathered wings scattered his sweet angel scent. His strong arm steadied her as he banked and slowed his descent. She didn't trust people in general, but she trusted him.

For the first time, Valka missed having wings. It would be a great advantage in battle, but Valkyries didn't have any. They flew on horses, geese, or dragons... and now, tigers.

The soft ocean breeze swayed the palms of the tall trees surrounding the massive landing pads. She marveled at the neat layout of the spaceport. Everything was square and massive, so unlike the architecture of circles and domes she'd seen in the angel town.

Something around the spaceport shimmered in the afternoon sun. "Is that a fence?"

"Yes." Konrad shaded his eyes. "A very high fence, but no domed ceiling... to allow for easy vertical landing and takeoff."

Ships of diverse construction and origin sat on the bare stone pads, like flocks of blue gems and silver ingots napping in the sun, twinkling as they reflected the warm rays.

Valka recognized old GTA transports, freighters, raptors, light fighters, shuttles, and battleships in various stages of refurbishing. A few ominous black ships reminded her of scorpions with deadly stingers. Interceptors and barracudas also clung to the platforms like enormous roaches, seemingly out of place on this peaceful planet. Smaller craft looked like luxury yachts equipped with hull cannons.

She estimated a thousand ships, on a hundred giant pads. "Are all these ships being refitted with angel technology?"

"Yes." Konrad hovered above the complex, as if to give her the best view. "We don't need to build ships. We just fix and adapt whatever crashed here to make it work with our technology."

Valka gazed over the vast spaceport, shading her eyes from the sun with her free hand. "That's a big fleet."

"This is just a tiny fraction of it." Konrad chuckled. "The bulk of our fleet is up in orbit, where it belongs, piloted by our androids and protecting Azura."

Valka noticed a massive round tower to the side, made of shiny metal. On close scrutiny, the tower was an amalgam of wrecked battleships, twisted, compacted, and melted into a tall cylindric shape... probably with the power of angel minds.

"Interesting recycling technique." She couldn't help teasing.

Konrad glanced at the tower then at her with a disapproving brow. "A monument to never forget the great battle we almost lost."

"Sorry." So, he didn't like to be teased about angel failures. Noted.

The *Blue Phantom* sat alone on its own platform, dwarfed by the gigantic stone block. As they flew closer, Valka realized the granite landing pads were low-truncated pyramids several klicks wide... each carved from a single block of stone. "These platforms are enormous. And they look old. What kind of ships were they built for?"

"Not ours. Something much bigger." Konrad deposited her on the flat granite, close to the *Blue Phantom*.

Very smooth landing. The sentinels lining the landing pad were so still, Valka almost didn't notice them. Straight as stone pillars, they stared into nothingness. Were they meditating? Visualizing? She focused on one of them and got her answer. They were searching for intruders with their minds.

Konrad nodded to the two guards standing in front of the *Blue Phantom's* belly ramp. Only one nodded back. The other kept staring into nothingness, still mentally scanning the area.

"So, if not the angels, who built that enormous spaceport?" She wanted to engage him, thirsty for his attention.

Konrad gave Valka a side glance. "A race of space-faring giants who lived here long ago."

"Did you say giants?" Valka realized she was still holding his arm and let go of it with reluctance. She straightened her weapons belt to give herself countenance. "So, the current angels weren't the first inhabitants of this special planet?"

"Far from it." Konrad's white feathered wings shrank and retracted. "Many races found and claimed this place over millions of cycles."

"Were the ancient giants also angels?" Valka tried to imagine colossal beings with wings and supernatural powers.

"Not at all." Konrad led the way up the lowered ramp of the *Blue Phantom*. "From the Akashic records we know the giants who built this place lived here long before the crystal took hold of Azura."

"Took hold?" Valka realized how little she knew. "The crystal wasn't always here?"

Konrad shook his head. "Sometime after the giants left, a small asteroid of pure Blue Crystal hit Azura's ocean, creating earthquakes and tidal waves, burying itself in the crust. Over time the crystal grew and interspersed with the other minerals in the ground. It's now an integral part of the planet core. It is the reason Azura glows in space."

"Like the crystal core of the *Blue Phantom* transformed it into a glowing ship?" It made sense. The crystal of Asgard was also alive and had many wonderful properties.

At the top of the ramp, Konrad returned the salute of the guard standing there, then he led the way toward the engine room. "It's also how the Byzantium Space Station turned from a galactic penitentiary and gambling hell into an angel hub, almost overnight."

Valka followed him along the tall, luminous corridors with crystal buttresses. "So, whoever landed on Azura after the crystal hit, became the first angels?"

"Yes." Konrad returned more angel salutes as they crossed a room full of monitors. "Except that these ships would have crashed, not landed."

"Because the crystal disables all electronics and conventional technology?" They kept a good clip along more corridors. Valka wondered why they didn't just dematerialize. Although, she rather liked walking with him in this dreamy glow that smelled like spring flowers.

"You get it." Konrad turned into a side corridor, narrower but still luminous with a high ceiling. "Unable to leave the planet, the survivors of many crashed ships would have formed a unique society, with enhanced longevity and supernatural powers."

She chuckled. "Good thing the universe doesn't know its revered angels are just an accident of nature."

"Maybe they are... or maybe not." Konrad raised his brow and flashed an enigmatic smile.

"What do you mean?" Valka enjoyed his mystery game. He was loosening his rigid attitude. Was it because of her? Or did Azura influence him?

Konrad slowed his steps. "Over time, under the guidance of the Formless One, the new angels learned to use their powers for the service of the greater good."

"The Formless One... again." Valka didn't quite trust the elusive spirit of the crystal.

"Yes. The Formless One speaks through the crystal." Konrad nodded. "Then the angels started to visualize beyond the confines of this planet, and manifested in different parts of the universe."

Valka remembered seeing statuettes of angels popping up in the souvenir shops in spaceports all over the galaxy. "That must be what started the fantastic stories the explorers told, about the Guardian Angels of the Universe."

"Yes." Konrad glanced back at her, with a mischievous glint in his eyes. "Want to see something very few have seen?"

"I'm intrigued." She enjoyed these stolen moments. He seemed like a different man since they landed on Azura... no longer somber, but happy.

"This way." Konrad walked to a massive hatch and waved at it. It started to lift, very slowly, making no sound.

"Later the angels carried crystal off planet, erected temples, and established a benevolent presence in the galaxy with angel friars and healing circles." Konrad watched the hatch still lifting.

"And now you are using the outreach temples to recruit new angels." Valka stepped into the blue glow of the engine room then she followed his gaze... up.

High overhead, nine crystal spheres floated in a slow circle and hummed in perfect harmony. The vibrations in that engine room were so strong, Valka could hear the musical harmonies and feel them deep inside her bones. "I've never seen an engine like this."

"You are looking at a power source that will never stop, never slow down, never fail... for as long as it is in place." Konrad's baritone voice hinted at pride. Odd for an angel. "And it all started with a crystal the size of a fist."

"Impressive. What happens when a weapon hits it? Would it explode? Blow up the ship?" That was always a possibility with formidable power sources.

"Explode?" The surprise on Konrad's handsome face was priceless. He seemed to be searching for information in his mind. "I don't think so. It would require an unimaginable force. I don't think such a force exists in our universe."

"What if that force came from another universe?" Encouraged by his friendly attitude, Valka enjoyed testing him. "Like Nyxifer..."

"I really do not know." He frowned. "Why are you asking? Your questions confuse me."

"In war times, one must consider all possibilities." Valka had nightmares about Asgard's magical core blasted to smithereens, in a shower of asteroids throughout the universe. Asgard, too, had precious crystal at its heart.

A shadow obscured Konrad's blue eyes and his shoulders fell. "The only time our ships failed was when the enemy used that special EMP weapon from another universe to neutralize our crystal. But nothing exploded. The ships just stalled dead in space, or fell from the sky, and crashed under the pull of gravity."

Valka sensed his pain and regretted going too far. "Sorry, I didn't mean to bring up bad memories."

"Whatever trials we go through make us what we are." He squared his shoulders. "Next on the tour, the new weapons we are installing on all our ships."

"The Nyxifer-killing weapons?"

"We call them NK weapons."

"Cool." Valka followed him out of the engine room. Unwilling to cause him more pain, she changed the topic. "Could you seed other planets with crystal to transform them into angel planets?"

"In theory, we could... with a chunk of crystal the size of a hill." He grunted. "But it would have to be a virgin planet with no technology."

"Why a virgin planet?" The musical vibration of the crystal engines faded as they walked away from the engine room and deeper into the ship.

"Besides creating natural upheavals, the crystal would disable whatever technology is already there, paralyzing the current civilization... like it did when it took over the Byzantium Space Station many cycles ago."

"So, your Blue Crystal could be used to cripple a technological planet?" Valka found this tidbit very interesting.

"In theory, with a large enough quantity, yes." Konrad flinched. Had he not foreseen such a possibility?

"I guess, power is power." Valka shook her head. "Even the most benign power source can be used as a weapon."

"That's why the angels have strict rules." Konrad's deep blue eyes stared into hers. "What makes our crystal safe is the integrity and righteousness of the angels who control it... and their dedication to the Formless One."

Valka could read all the way to his soul. He still loved and worshipped rules. "What would happen if an angel broke the sacred rules and did something unspeakable?"

"The other angels would neutralize and isolate the rogue individual." The armory hatch lifted, and Konrad stepped into the weapons hold with a resolute stride.

"You would lock the rogue angel in one of your power-dampening cells?" Valka followed him inside the smaller room, remembering how powerless she had felt, stuck in such a cell.

"We do what is necessary." Konrad motioned to the shelves of perfectly aligned hand weapons. All of them glowed blue. "These new NK blasters are capable of killing the kind of entity that might come from the universe that sent us Nyxor a few cycles ago, and now this evil Nyxifer... if they are from the same place."

"Why so many weapons?" Valka thought the entity was singular. "Are you expecting more than one evil being?"

"Last time, it was only one, but he could give extraordinary powers to his minions and summon legions of demons. This time, we do not know how many entities might come from their universe of origin." Konrad straightened a blaster out of line on the bulkhead shelf. "In the past, such entities could also turn our androids against us."

"Not a good thing. Fortunately, you now have plenty of new angel recruits." Valka caressed one large blaster. It hummed under her touch.

"Careful. These are made for angel hands." Konrad picked one up and admired it. "Only angels can use them. Their contact could be detrimental to non-angels."

"They feel warm." Valka couldn't help being attracted to these blasters. She wanted one. But Konrad would not agree to it, and she couldn't steal one under his watchful gaze. Besides, stealing was probably against angel rules.

"Maybe these weapons don't sting you because you are wearing your crystal pendant..." Konrad reached and caressed her pendant.

She could read his mind screaming he wished her to become an angel. Could Valka be changing from all the crystal on Azura? No. Impossible. Still, she wanted one of those special blasters. "Can we try shooting one?"

"Not here. They are very destructive." He shook his head. "And these weapons wouldn't obey your mind or your touch anyway."

"Right. I'm not an angel." Still, Valka believed this could be the perfect weapon for her. As if it called to her.

Konrad froze and stared in the distance, listening. "I have to go. My light transport is ready."

Valka's mind also caught the mental message. "Right. You have to pick up that batch of volunteers from the temple on Carina Prime."

He offered her his hand. "Want to come and see me off?"

"Sure." She took his hand and experienced the tingles of dematerialization... slightly different from when she did it. But she enjoyed the contact of his warm skin, the strength of his arm. It made her heart sing.

They rematerialized several landing pads away, in front of a light transport. The relatively small ship shimmered and glowed blue, like all angel ships. She let go of his arm with reluctance.

"I wish I could go with you." She allowed her voice to trail with regret.

"I won't be long. I promise. Stay here and learn about Azura." His strangled voice indicated strong emotions as well. "I'll be back by morning and pick you up for more sightseeing."

"I'd like that." Valka knew he couldn't voice his true feelings, but she was glad the separation bothered him, too. For some reason, the idea of Konrad leaving made her uncomfortable. She hoped it was just the manifestation of her silly crush on him.

Konrad inclined his head and smiled as he vanished. Within seconds, the light transport rose, hovered above the stone pad, then simply dematerialized.

Valka took a last look at the spaceport. The sun was lower in the sky. Konrad said to keep Sultan inside the compound at night. Although the tiger could take care of himself, she didn't want him to get lost or feel abandoned.

She transported herself to the beach and shaded her eyes to scan the long strip of golden sand. In the distance, she spotted the tiger frolicking in the waves with other cats about his size.

She stopped walking and whistled a few notes. "Sultan!"

The tiger raised his head then raced toward her, strong muscles springing and stretching with his powerful stride.

Valka sat on the beach, easing the weapons on her belt. Then she faced the ebbing waves glistening pink as they reflected the rays of the setting sun. She relaxed and inhaled the salty breeze.

The tiger closed the distance, then head-bumped her shoulder;

"I see you made some friends." She was grateful he did.

"*Yes.*" The big cat sat next to her. "*Sultan like Azura.*"

"I like it, too, Sweetheart." How Valka missed Asgard. She'd been alone for so long. How she wished for a place to call home, a place to belong, with people who loved her like family.

Her mind returned to Konrad. He was growing on her. She liked him more and more... but she couldn't let herself fall in love... ever.

* * *

Konrad visualized the landing strip near the glowing dome of the Azuran temple on Carina Prime. He fell off his levitating meditation, and down onto the crystal bench above which he had been floating. What happened? Did something hit the transport? The crystal drive no longer hummed. Impossible.

Several alarms rang all over the ship like bells and gongs, then utter silence. Weird. He felt heavy on his legs. His attempt at dematerialization failed. So, he ran along the short corridor to the control room.

No one at the controls. All the monitors stood dark. The natural glow of the ship gradually dimmed then died. Everything was black and cold. It seemed they were dead in space, but where?

Closing his eyes to see through the darkness, Konrad realized he could no longer visualize. Why? Even the crystal implanted at the base of his neck had gone dark and felt like a cold lump. Tendrils of fear snaked through his body.

Konrad remembered with dread the EMP technology that had knocked down Azura's defenses in one strike. Was that what happened here? He heard a bang close by, and heavy steps. The transport had been boarded.

He was a sitting duck in the dark. Could he still make himself invisible?

Something heavy hit his head, and he lost consciousness.

* * *

Konrad came to when a booted foot kicked his ribs, and he moaned. His head also hurt. A strange musty smell reached his nostrils... along with blood... and smoke. Through half-closed lids he spied his surroundings. His captors were humanoid brutes in black armor.

His bound hands and feet went numb as the black clad soldiers dragged him over the uneven floor paved with rough stones. Heavy gravity indicated a planet. The dim, yellow glow of flickering torches bathed the cave-like space.

He focused to read his captors' minds... in vain. Sharp pain hit his wrists and ankles.

Then the black armored soldiers threw him into a small nook enclosed by bars and slammed the sliding gate. The loud metallic clunk indicated a strong lock. After his jailors walked away, Konrad focused on loosening his bonds, mentally at first, then by turning his hands. But it didn't work, and the cuffs stung him again.

Acclimating his eyes to the dim glow, he realized his cuffs and ankle restraints were made of metal, and highly technological, with dials and electronic indicators. He attempted to make himself invisible but failed. He couldn't dematerialize either. Another jolt stung him.

It seemed his attackers used power dampening technology. A cold shudder of recognition ran down his spine. He must send a message to Azura. They could trace him, free him from whatever evil he'd fallen victim to... except that he could no longer communicate with his mind. Drats!

The look of the walls and floor, and the dim orange glow, reminded him of the holographic meeting he'd witnessed with the heads of the Priory. Could he be in their stronghold? Could the angel spy who transmitted the secret meeting still be here? Could Konrad make contact? Or had the angel spy been found and neutralized, like him?

What a filthy prison. A dirty mat, a stinky piss pot, soiled rags from the previous occupant. The smoke of many torches and the metallic smell of blood made him want to vomit. In the distance, ominous drums punctuated a lugubrious chant.

The crystal at the base of his neck awakened and pulsed. Konrad allowed himself to hope. Maybe now, he could call for help. As he attempted to contact Azura, his mind refused to focus. His cuffs beeped and sent a paralyzing signal along his arms. He flinched.

Drats! Although he no longer detected the strange EMP that paralyzed his ship, he realized the electronic cuffs did more than restrain his wrists. They also neutralized his abilities, and sent pain signals when he tried to use them.

He thought about Valka, glad he didn't bring her along on this trip. He understood how alone and powerless she must have felt in her power-dampening cage on Pandemonium. But he must not give in to fear.

Regardless of his angel abilities, Konrad was still a trained supersoldier... although the stinging cuffs seemed also to be delivering some kind of drug to dull body and mind. He could feel the poison invading his veins. Still, he would find a way out. They would have to come get him sometime. And he would be ready. If only he could get rid of the cuffs...

Chapter Eleven

In the dim cave, incense smoke swirled, infernal drums beat a frenzied rhythm, and chanting filled the high vaults. Black clad Abbotts and other faceless worshipers in neat rows bowed as they repeated an obscure litany in a long-lost language.

On the altar stone, a man, cuffed to the altar spread eagle, struggled and moaned in agony. He shrieked at the sight of the sacrificial blade poised above him. Then the shiny metal flashed and the blade dropped, piercing his chest, splitting ribs.

Crimson blood spurted then flowed out of the man's open mouth, and arterial jets splattered the black mask and robes of the officiating Abbott. The victim's wide eyes, fixed on the ceiling, stopped seeing. The Abbott's murderous hands reached inside the man's chest, shattering ribs, then pulled out the still beating heart and ripped it from his body.

The faceless Abbott raised the dripping heart above his head.

From a swirl of red smoke emerged a tall, naked entity with crimson skin and gleaming ram horns... a hermaphrodite, both male and female.

The officiant bowed. "Exalted Master, Lord Nyxifer, Bringer of Darkness! Accept this small offering. We welcome your reign in this universe."

The naked entity took the bloody heart, examined it, then bit into it with gusto. The dripping blood ran like clear water on the red skin.

"All hail Nyxifer!" The officiating Abbott shouted.

"All hail Nyxifer!" Abbotts and worshipers repeated in unison. "All hail Nyxifer! All hail Nyxifer!"

"No!" Valka thrashed on her bed in cold sweat, tangled in the sheets. She couldn't wake up. She wanted the nightmare to stop. She screamed.

A raspy tongue licked her face. *"Sultan here. Sultan protect."*

Tossing the sheets, Valka sat upright, panting, eyes wide open. Her heart still racing to the frenzied rhythm of the drums in her nightmare. She gasped for air. As she checked her surroundings, she realized she was on Azura, and all was normal. Steady rain drummed on the Blue Crystal dome, and lightning flashed outside, illuminating the inside of her temporary residence with blue shadows.

But what had scared Valka wasn't just a bad dream. It wasn't a vision from the Valkyries either. Somehow, she knew Konrad was in grave and imminent danger.

The crystal pendant on her chest pulsed softly. How odd. As she took the crystal in her hands and focused on the pulse, she could feel Konrad, out in the universe. She knew exactly where he was. Somehow, her secret feelings for him must link them together.

Closing her eyes, she could see him, unconscious, in a cell. He was in the Priory stronghold on Taurus Secundus. The Abbotts were holding Konrad and would sacrifice him next. She was certain of it. Her blood ran cold at the very thought.

She couldn't imagine a world without Konrad. She wouldn't let him die horribly for the sake of that red devil. She must save him.

Sultan head-bumped her shoulder. *"Sultan protect."*

She patted the big cat. "Sweetheart, we have to save Angel Konrad. He is in great danger."

The tiger harrumphed. *"Puny Angel Konrad need help?"*

"Yes. But we can't just show up and hope to succeed. My Valkyrie powers aren't enough to face that kind of enemy. We need a ship with big guns, the Nyxifer-killing kind." And Valka knew exactly where to find one.

She thought of waking the angels to tell them, but it was the middle of the night, and they would likely want her to wait. They would want to consult each-other, deliberate, weigh the consequences, study all the angles, maybe consult the Formless One, then vote and decide according to their complicated rules.

There was no time for rules. Valka would leave them a message, but she couldn't wait. Konrad needed help now.

* * *

Ignoring the downpour, Valka marched into the garden adjacent to her dome, followed by Sultan. No one in sight. The heavy rain would provide cover. Konrad had mentioned large predators in the jungle at night, so she would avoid it.

She leapt on Sultan's back. "We'll rematerialize high in the air and fly to the spaceport. I'll show you the way."

"Sultan help Valka." The tiger flapped his wings.

Valka dematerialized the two of them and they manifested beyond the confines of the shield, high above the agglomeration of glowing blue domes. The battering rain made it difficult for Sultan to fly, and for her to see far, but it would conceal their flight.

A lightning strike hit the metal blades and blasters hanging from Valka's belt and zinged her a little. "By Odin's beard!"

"Ouch! Sultan hit." The tiger dropped a few meters.

Valka patted his neck. "Steady, Sweetheart."

"Sultan okay." The tiger quickly recovered and now flew in a straight line, North-East, toward the spaceport.

Good thing her armor could absorb high voltage. Hopefully, lightning wouldn't strike twice.

Valka would have to be stealthy, so she made herself invisible to the guards' eyes... and to their searching minds. Fortunately, the downpour added another layer of camouflage. Perfect.

As the faint illuminations of the spaceport appeared in the distance through the sheets of rain, the strange sound of many flapping wings mixed with the wet clatter of the downpour.

Something big and heavy pulled Sultan's right wing down. The tiger went spiraling toward the ground.

Valka hung on to Sultan and joined her mind to his. "Easy, Sweetheart." She helped him recover his balance. "What happened?"

"Big bird. Many bird." The tiger now flew straight, regaining altitude.

"Birds?" Valka realized that in this land of large predators, some of them might have wings.

A brief moon ray between the clouds revealed a flock of giant birds, like black vultures, surrounding them and pecking at Sultan. Her invisibility cloak didn't fool the birds. They must be guided by smell. The tiger snapped his jaws and lashed with his tail, expelling raindrops from his fur. Feathers from his wings scattered in the rain.

Valka threw silver stars and hit her marks. Three giant vultures fell back, wounded, but this was a large flock... and they seemed ravenous.

Desperate situations called for desperate measures. But the Azurans respected their wildlife, and so did Valka. Focusing her powers, she grew a protective bubble around her and the flying tiger. The bubble pushed the birds farther and farther away, then it exploded and stunned all the vultures, throwing them a klick away in every direction... but they were only disoriented, and they might return.

She patted the tiger's injured neck, stopping the bleeding and infusing him with healing energy. "Hurry, Sweetheart."

"Sultan hurry." The tiger flapped his wings harder, but he was weaker on one side.

Valka applied her hand to the wet fur, sending Sultan more healing energy.

She hoped her invisibility cloak would prevent detection from the guards at the spaceport, and she focused to shield herself and sultan from their minds. A simple task for her, but she'd never used these abilities on angels before, and they tended to be more perceptive than ordinary people.

The rain abated somewhat, and she had a panoramic view of the dimly lit spaceport, where the stone platforms, wet from the downpour, reflected the moonlight.

"To the left, Sultan." She leaned left, directing Sultan past the *Blue Phantom,* toward the landing pad holding the luxury yachts recently equipped with the new weapons. One yacht in particular seemed to be more heavily armed than the others. She pointed to it. "This one."

"Sultan see." The tiger swooped down through the rain toward the yacht.

Although her invisibility of eyes and mind camouflage should work, Valka added a cloud of confusion, affecting all the angels in the vicinity of the spaceport... just in case. Stealing was against their rules, and she didn't want to be arrested. It would cause delays, and nothing should interfere with her mission. She must save Konrad from a horrible fate.

The rain all but stopped as the tiger landed near the larger yacht bristling with big guns. The name on the hull read *Sweet Freedom.* How appropriate.

None of the guards on the platform perimeter reacted. Good. Valka's invisibility cloak was working.

Bright lights came on above a neighboring platform, attracting the guards' attention. A ship was coming down on approach, high above, preparing for a vertical landing. Perfect. It would distract the guards while she stole the yacht.

She vaulted off the tiger, walked to the yacht, applied her hands on the hatch and focused her mind. The panel lifted, and she and Sultan boarded the *Sweet Freedom.* It was dark inside. No one onboard. Good.

"Lights!" Valka's heart rejoiced when the ship responded to her command. Lights and monitors came to life.

On close inspection of the control panel, all the cannons were equipped with the new weapons, and several hand guns of the Nyxifer-killing kind stood on the weapons racks. There must be more in the armory. This was the ship she needed.

She walked to the control room, followed by Sultan. Then she sat in the captain's chair. The big cat sat on the deck next to her chair by the consoles.

Projecting her mind outside the ship, Valka ascertained the guards' attention remained on the arriving vessel on the adjacent mega-platform. Then she focused her mind and dematerialized the *Sweet Freedom* to rematerialize it into deep space.

Done. "We are in free galactic space, Sweetheart. You can relax for a while."

The tiger licked his injured wing. *"Sultan rest."*

After scanning with her mind to make sure no one had followed her, Valka refocused to send a mind message to Captain Graziella, of the *Blue Phantom*.

"Captain, General Konrad Lagarde is detained on Taurus Secundus and scheduled to be ritually sacrificed by the Priory. The Nyxifer entity is on the premises. I'm on my way and could use some backup."

She released the mind message and let it fly toward the captain of the *Blue Phantom*. She hoped Graziella the Merciful valued Konrad enough to persuade the Azurans to come to his rescue.

* * *

When heavy bootsteps on stone penetrated his stupor, Konrad sat up, but he felt dizzy, struggling to focus. His head pounded with each beat of his heart. He barely remembered being dragged to this filthy cell. His memories seemed fuzzy. He'd lost track of time. Had he been drugged? He might have lost consciousness for a while.

The rusty gate slid open with a metallic grind. Big, tough mercenaries in black armor, with full helmets hiding their faces marched in, blasters pointed at him. Rough hands pulled him up to his feet.

As a genetically enhanced super-soldier, Konrad should be able to handle them... but he was weak, unbalanced, unable to support his own weight. The blinking cuffs on his wrists did more than just cancel his special abilities. The drugs they released were sapping his strength. They also made it difficult for him to think straight.

As his captors half-dragged, half-carried him along dimly lit tunnels, Konrad struggled to remember. His light transport had been neutralized and taken. His captors weren't space pirates, but part of an organized military unit with the latest technology. Then he remembered the strange vibration that disabled his small transport.

This was the same EMP technology that made Azura's ships fall from the sky during the last battle... technology from Nyxifer's universe. Azura had developed new weapons against him, but the strange EMP problem remained unsolved.

Then the reality of his condition hit him. He was helpless in enemy hands. "Where are we going?"

"Walk!" A black soldier shoved him forward with a grunt.

Konrad stumbled, feigning extreme weakness. His balance was slowly returning along with his memories, as his supersoldier body fought the toxins, but he didn't want his jailors to know it. He was underground, in what looked like the Priory stronghold he'd seen through the angel spy's mind. And the smoke and litanies coming from the opening ahead of them augured bad things.

The Abbotts were behind this... and they had help. Their evil master gave them the technology to defeat the angels– the same EMP device that defeated Azura before. Drats!

Konrad shuddered as old memories of power-hungry despots resurfaced. They gained supremacy through blood sacrifices, by spreading terror. And the man now leading the Priory was the worst of them all...

Admiral Krow, Killer Krow, his treacherous former boss. The man who had betrayed him, framed him for treason, and sentenced him to death cycles ago.

How he wished he'd killed him the day he inflicted those scars. But fate intervened. Somehow, Killer Krow survived. And now Konrad was about to die before he could complete his mission.

As they neared an arched entrance, the chant intensified, with drums beating a fast tempo. Konrad's heart raced in his chest. He struggled with the cold fear coursing through his veins. He knew what would come next. He'd seen it before. But he was restrained, hands and feet, with no angel powers and diminished strength.

Something hard hit his head from behind. He fell under the splitting pain, then his captors dragged him over the cave floor, half-conscious. Strong hands lifted his body, his wrists came apart, and he was forced down, spread eagle on a flat stone, ankles and wrists electronically fastened to the four corners of the altar. All he could see was the cave ceiling, where smoke swirled in the orange glow of the flickering torches.

The crystal at the base of his throat pulsed softly, in sync with another crystal... Valka... if only she knew... but he was glad she wasn't here. At least she would be spared.

The officiating Abbott considered him for a few seconds, as if savoring the moment.

Konrad stared into the eyes behind the black mask and shuddered with recognition. He would know that cold black stare anywhere. It was Killer Krow himself, his former boss, the man who framed him and wanted him dead.

Konrad closed his eyes briefly to control his fear and slow his heartbeat. He smelled the blood of former sacrifices, and tasted copper in his mouth. Unable to call for help in his mind, he was doomed. Time to pay for his past sins...

But angels did not fear death. It wasn't the end, but a portal to another beginning. Besides, he wouldn't let evil feed on his fear. Konrad relaxed and found peace as he accepted his fate. Time for his soul to join the Formless One.

Chapter Twelve

On Azura, aboard the *Blue Phantom* parked at the spaceport, Captain Graziella the Merciful awoke in the middle of the night in her private quarters. As her eyes adapted to the soft glow of her cabin, a telepathic message echoed in her mind.

"Captain, this is Valka. General Konrad Lagarde is detained on Taurus Secundus and scheduled to be ritually sacrificed by the Priory. The Nyxifer entity is on the premises. I'm on my way and could use some backup."

Graziella sat up and closed her eyes to broadcast the message to all the angels on Azura, then she gently shook the lovely woman sleeping at her side. "Leana? Wake up, my love."

Her lover stirred then sat up, stretched her wings and retracted them. She looked so beautiful in white silk, svelte, with soft amber skin and long dark hair in disarray.

"What's happening?" Leana froze as the collective message unfolded in her mind. "The General is in deep trouble on the Priory stronghold? Nyxifer is there, too..." Her clear blue eyes opened wide. "Nyxifer?"

"Yes, my sweet love. We must rally Azura's armed forces to fight that evil entity." Graziella stepped off the wide bunk bed, dropped her silk robe, and grabbed a white uniform from the bulkhead shelf. "It's all happening on Taurus Secundus."

The lovely Leana scrambled out of bed and pulled fresh clothes from the shelf as well. "But the *Blue Phantom* is not battle ready, yet."

"Not quite, but most of the new weapons are online." Graziella zipped up her uniform to the high collar then raked back her short blond hair with slender fingers. "It will have to do."

Another message, this one from the Council, reached Graziella's mind. *"Emergency officers' briefing in the main temple."*

Her lover's blue eyes widened. "What was that?"

"The Council is going to consult the Formless One." Graziella kissed her on the forehead. "Recall the crew. Prepare the ship for battle. Make sure we are ready to transport troops and fly as soon as we get the official order."

"Aye, aye, Captain." Leana drawled the words and tilted her head, then pulled down Graziella's shirt zipper a few inches and trailed her finger down between her breasts.

Graziella gasped at the sensual touch but resisted the invitation. "And none of that familiar attitude toward the captain in front of the crew, please." She smiled to soften the rebuke. "Understood?"

"Understood, Captain." Leana gazed at her with soft blue eyes full of love.

Graziella kissed her lover's forehead again. Then she straightened and pulled up her zipper before dematerializing on her way to the temple. Duty called.

* * *

Valka manifested in the evil temple, high above the altar, on Sultan's back, under cover of invisibility. A red glow enveloped everything. Taking in the scene, she gasped. Helshades! The shiny blade of the sacrificial dagger was poised above Konrad's bare chest, and the Abbott recited some archaic litany in a long-lost language.

Valka struggled to slow her heartbeat as she drew her favorite blaster and fired. The blade flew out of the officiant's hand across the space, far from his reach.

A murmur of surprise from the crowd, then black clad soldiers posted at the entrances rushed into the sanctum, searching for the culprit on the ground. Good luck!

Valka couldn't let them see her. She must save Konrad before they killed him. Was her aim good enough to shatter his restraints without hurting him? She fired and missed, then adjusted her aim. Three more shots, and Konrad was free, but he wasn't moving. By Odin's beard! What did they do to him?

She swooped down to collect him, but as she neared the altar, some unexpected vibration disrupted her invisibility cloak. The crowd exclaimed at the sight of her on Sultan, and the black soldiers rushed toward the altar, aiming their blasters in her direction.

Helshades! Valka activated a bubble shield to protect Sultan from blasters and projectiles.

Leaning over to grab Konrad's arm, Valka then lifted him across Sultan's back.

The tiger shuddered under the hail of blaster fire breaking on the bubble shield. *"Sultan heavy, not fly."*

"Let's dematerialize, then." Valka hoped she could.

In a swirl of red smoke, a naked Nyxifer with gleaming white horns rose from the ground. Red fire sprang out of his extended hands. He pointed one hand at Valka.

Valka focused to dematerialize, but the shot of red fire shocked her, sending the three of them flying against the cave wall. They bounced, thanks to the bubble shield. Seeing her opportunity, Valka seized the special Azuran weapon and fired at Nyxifer. The NK weapon did not fire. Nothing happened. By Loki's balls!

And Nyxifer was still blasting her bubble shield with red energy beams.

Valka shook Konrad and placed the weapon in his hands. "Wake up! You fire it. You are an angel. I'm not."

Konrad seemed to understand. He grasped the blue blaster, aimed and fired, but the bubble shield burst under Nyxifer's persistent energy blasts, sending them reeling. Konrad missed. He fired again but Nyxifer moved out of the way and the blast hit the pillar behind him.

Then Konrad collapsed. Helshades!

Nyxifer targeted them again, aiming his red energy beam toward them.

Under fire from all sides by soldiers, without her shield, Valka focused harder to vanish. She dematerialized the three of them and rematerialized them aboard the angel yacht, invisible in space. Once in the relative safety of the ship, she remembered to breathe. But they couldn't stay here.

Konrad looked unconscious, next to Sultan lying flat on the deck of the control room.

As Valka focused her mind to dematerialize the yacht, a red glow surrounded them. Projecting her mind into space, she saw Nyxifer's giant image floating in the void, enveloping the yacht in a luminous red ball of strange energy. She ordered the special Azuran weapons on the ship to fire on the red entity, but the weapons didn't obey her command... Helshades! She wasn't an angel.

The ship banked hard and Konrad rolled on the deck as Sultan gripped the soft decking with his claws to stay anchored. Then the yacht started to spin. Valka seized the arms of the pilot chair and strapped herself in. Then everything whirled around her.

Closing her eyes, she saw in her mind a rip opening in black space, and her yacht slipped through the portal. Then she found herself falling, falling, as if the fall would never end.

When the ship finally stabilized, Valka's heart was beating so fast, she thought it would burst. What happened? Where were they? Where had the entity propelled them? Valka had the eerie feeling that something terrible had happened.

Konrad was wedged at the corner of deck and bulkhead. Sultan was throwing up on the soft decking.

She ran to Konrad and checked his pulse... normal. He was knocked out but breathing normally. Good. His angel constitution would bring him back quickly.

She ran to the tiger who'd retched his last meal. "Sultan? Are you okay, Sweetheart?"

The tiger moaned in response. *"Sultan hiccup. Sultan okay."*

Valka breathed a sigh of relief.

She projected her mind outside the ship to take her bearings and realized it was orbiting a red planet. The instruments on the yacht didn't recognize it.

She didn't either. "Computer, extrapolate an explanation for where we are."

"We are not in the known universe." The computer beeped. "We may be in a hidden or uncharted part of the fringe, or... somehow we slipped through a portal, into another universe."

"Another universe?" Valka's heart beat a fierce tempo. "By Thor's hammer! What now?"

* * *

Konrad grimaced and shook his head to scatter the butterflies fluttering in his mind. He was free of his bonds, on the control deck of a small angel ship. He'd regained his full abilities, he felt strong again. He gagged at the acidic smell of vomit.

A few feet away, Sultan groomed himself and growled a warning in his direction. Would the cat ever warm up to him?

In the captain's chair, Valka looked stunned as she stared at the monitors. Konrad rejoiced at seeing her unscathed.

"Thanks for rescuing me." His voice broke and he cleared his throat. "Are you alright? What happened?"

"I'm fine. Welcome back." Her quick smile vanished. "But it looks like the Nyxifer entity threw us into another universe." She sounded dumbfounded.

"What?" Konrad rose to his feet and stared at the control panel.

The images of the red planet they orbited showed cities, streets, and buildings attesting to a sophisticated civilization. A close-up revealed an entire population of naked red people with ram-like horns, very similar to the Nyxor of old, and the new Nyxifer entity.

"This must be their planet of origin... in a different universe." Konrad now started to understand the incredible power Nyxifer possessed.

"Why would he send us to his home?" Valka shook her head. "Do you think they are all alike? Bloodthirsty and power-hungry?"

"If that's the case, he sent us here to die." Konrad shuddered at the very thought of an entire population of evil entities. "Can they see us?"

"No. Stealth mode is active." Valka's peridot green eyes seemed wider than before. "What do we do now?"

"Get information." Konrad was glad for his military training. "Maybe this universe has an Akashic record like ours."

"The universal record of all knowledge?" She nodded her understanding. "Cool."

"Let's see what I can find out."

"Okay." Her voice regained some confidence.

The tiger lay on the deck, paws crossed in a relaxing pose but kept a keen eye on Konrad.

Konrad sat in midair and closed his eyes. "Focus with me so you can see it, too."

"Right. But I'd rather stay on the chair." Valka relaxed and crossed her legs in the captain's chair.

In front of them, Konrad's mind projected images of a different world with a different history, vastly different people, and many different planets. This planet was Tangu. Once, there had been angels in this universe, fighting for the balance of good and evil. But Nyxor and Nyxifer had joined together to exterminate them and had destroyed their planet as well. There were no angels left to fight evil here.

Eventually, the people had revolted against the two tyrants, and banished them forever.

"So, the people of this universe are not evil. That's a relief." Valka sighed. "They may not want to kill us... and they might know how to get us back home."

"I'm not so sure. Look." Konrad focused on the images portraying the banishment of the two evil entities.

In front of them surged pictures of a crowd chanting as the two evil beings gradually lost consistency. At first, the foreign words made no sense, then the meaning came to light. "We banish you to the depths of hell. Be cursed to wander between universes for all eternity, forever unable to materialize as solid beings in any of them.

Valka sighed. "So, their people didn't send them to a particular universe, they just banished them from all physical universes."

"That's why these two do not have a tangible body in our universe. They manipulate other people to do their bidding. That's why our angels couldn't kill Nyxor. All they could do was banish him."

"At least, he can never return to our universe." Valka sounded relieved.

"But after Nyxor failed to destroy Azura and its angels, he sent his buddy Nyxifer to finish the job." Konrad wondered which one was worse. They came from the same place and had similar methods. But the new entity had probably learned much from the first incursion. Nyxifer had come prepared.

"Do you think Nyxifer can exterminate our angels?" Valka shook her head. "After all, they did succeed in their universe."

As if sensing her sadness, Sultan rubbed his big head against Valka's hand, and she obliged him with a scratch. Those two had a special bond. Konrad sometimes envied the tiger. No wonder the beast saw him as a rival for Valka's affections.

"Don't worry. Now that Azura has developed a Nyxifer-killing weapon, we might be able to put an end to their evil interference for good." Konrad certainly hoped so.

"Except that we are stuck here." Valka's flaxen braids brushed her lovely face as she turned to him. "Maybe forever."

Forever. What a concept. Konrad wasn't sure how he felt about not finishing the job and leaving his brothers to deal with Nyxifer. "We have to find a way to help our universe from this end."

Valka sighed. "What else do the Akashic records say about these two evil ones?"

Konrad refocused his mind, and more scenes from the past came to light. An unknown voice narrated the images:

"The two evil doers draw their special powers from the temple of the Dark Light, a source they discovered on a fiery planet while exploring the fringe. There is a black pillar of energy inside an ancient temple, buried deep under layers of molten lava. But many hot volcanic planets are scattered along the fringe. The people of Tangu searched for that source of evil power in hopes to destroy it, but they never found it. It's also said that the temple of the Dark Light is defended by demons."

As the images stopped, Konrad took a deep breath. "The mission doesn't end because we are stranded here. We have to find that temple and destroy that pillar of Dark Light."

"I agree." Valka's brow furrowed in a determined expression.

The big cat looked straight at Konrad in challenge. *"Sultan fight evil."*

"Glad we are all on the same page, for a change." Konrad smiled inside. He would tame that cat eventually. "If our special weapons can destroy that source of dark power, it will weaken Nyxifer and his acolytes, and might make them vulnerable in all universes."

"I hope so." Valka pursed her lips. "And maybe we should avoid interfering with the local population. Even if they are not evil, they might consider us a threat... especially since we carry weapons that are deadly to them."

"Agreed." Hope rose again in Konrad's chest.

"But the fringe is vast. It goes all the way around the galaxy. How are we going to find it?" Valka's forehead creased in concentration.

"Sultan help." The tiger sounded proud in Konrad's mind.

Konrad felt renewed at the prospect of fighting evil and helping his brothers in his universe. "Together we'll find and destroy that temple of the Dark Light."

Chapter Thirteen

"All clear so far." Konrad took a deep breath. At least they weren't under attack.

The monitors on the control deck of the *Sweet Freedom* purred. The stealth mode indicator blinked, and no one in this strange universe seemed to have detected their intrusion. The red planet below remained peaceful.

"Any idea how we are going to find that temple of the Dark Light?" Valka paced back and forth on the control deck, between the console and the tiger, who looked like a live Sphynx. "If only we had a scanner capable of locating this dark energy source..."

"Maybe we do." Konrad remembered something about the newly added weapons. "The NK weapons are geared to not just kill, but also sense and target evil entities from this strange universe."

Valka stopped pacing. "You mean, the new weapons are selective?"

"Kind of." Konrad leaned against the console and crossed his arms on his chest. It helped him think. "They'll strike anything we aim at, but they are also tuned to seek and destroy the specific Nyxor/Nyxifer vibration. And that particular vibration must also come from their unique power source."

Valka chewed her lip as if in deep thought. "Maybe we can recalibrate these new weapons and expand their reach to detect the kind of evil it's attuned to, but from a greater distance…"

"It might work." Konrad allowed himself a flicker of hope. "I imagine the vibrations of the Dark Light must be powerful and far-reaching… if you know what particular signal to search for."

The tiger yawned. *"Sultan tired."*

"You go ahead, Sweetheart." Valka patted the cat's head. "We don't need you right now."

"Sultan sleep." The tiger flopped on his side, emitted a big sigh, then started snoring.

"Lucky tiger." Konrad tried to keep his tone light, but he meant it.

Valka chuckled and shook her head. "Cats will use any opportunity to take a nap."

"About those weapons…" The beginning of a solution germinated in Konrad's mind. "Recalibrating the big cannons on the hull might be our best chance to detect that temple."

"We could point them in various directions, rotate the ship slowly to cover more ground, and wait for the signal." Valka plopped into the captain's chair. "Can you do the modifications?"

"I think I can." Konrad hoped he could deliver. "But I'll need your help."

"You've got it." Her smile at being needed illuminated the entire deck. "What do you need me to do?"

"Here... let me show you." Konrad pointed to a monitor on the wall.

* * *

On Azura, Graziella the Merciful stared at the large crystal floating high, near the dome of the main temple. The blue glow enveloped the twelve Android angels levitating in a circle around it in meditation mode. They seemed to purr as they channeled the energy of the Formless One.

On both sides of Graziella, all the fleet captains and Avenging angel officers stood at attention, in a wide circle around the central altar. A soft symphony of mellow sounds swirled in the air, along with the sweet scent of flowers and incense.

Standing at the altar, the Great Lady of Azura in flowing blue veils, raised her glowing sword to the crystal. "O Formless One, we seek your advice on the eve of battle. How can we best defeat this new threat to our universe?"

A bright flash from the crystal made everything in the temple glow... even the people. Graziella's heart beat faster. The Formless One had heard them.

One of the floating Androids turned away from the crystal, blinked, then spoke.

"This moment is pivotal in your mission to preserve the balance of good and evil." The deep thundering voice of the Formless One was startling coming from an Android.

"But the Nyxifer entity is particularly strong, and a threat for all universes. Unbeknownst to you, you are getting help from a faraway world. Line up your battleships around the evil stronghold but stay hidden, and wait for their signal."

"What signal, O Formless One?" The Great Lady's voice choked. She sounded worried.

"You will know when it happens." The thundering voice of the Formless One faded into infinity, and the channeling Android blinked back to meditation mode and turned to face the crystal.

The Great Lady of Azura lowered her sword and took a few breaths. Then she addressed the assembled officers. "You have your orders. To Taurus Secundus. Prepare for battle."

Graziella shivered. She had a bad feeling about this particular fight. She hoped the new weapons would give them the advantage, but angels had been defeated before, and there were no guaranties.

She also wondered about General Konrad Lagarde, prisoner on Taurus Secundus. With no new message from Valka, she could only hope he was still alive. But she couldn't worry about the welfare of one individual while the fate of the universe was at stake. Even if it was her first officer. She must focus all her energy on destroying Nyxifer.

* * *

Aboard the Sweet Freedom, Valka readjusted the direction of the hull cannons. Monitors showed the heavy cylinders slowly pivoting on their axes, to point in ten different directions. Grateful for Konrad's knowledge of Angel technology and his efficient recalibration, Valka locked the cannons then swiped the console, rebooting the entire system with the enhanced searching modification. "Done!"

Konrad joined her at the controls and stood close as they stared at the monitor wall, waiting for a ping.

"There!" Valka couldn't hide her excitement as she pointed at one monitor with a blinking red light. On the small screen, the straight echo lines now wavered like crawling worms. "It's faint, but it's definitely the right frequency."

Konrad narrowed his eyes at the wall of monitors. "Set course for the North-Eastern fringe. We'll follow that ping to its source."

"Aye, aye, Captain." Valka enjoyed working with Konrad. Despite all their differences, they understood each other and would get the job done.

Within minutes, the *Sweet Freedom* rematerialized in the vicinity of a small planetoid, red with volcanic activity. Bright rivers of lava alternated with black rock. Violent eruptions popped intermittently. The smoky atmosphere registered hot and highly toxic. Not a friendly environment for life. The scanners indicated a high intensity vibration coming from deep inside the planetoid.

"This is the right spot, according to the scanners, but I see no temple, no life, and no activity on the surface." Valka couldn't hide her disappointment. "Of course, it's never that easy."

"The Dark Light is probably deep underground." Konrad punched a few keys on the console. "Evil thrives in darkness, like the Priory in the caves of Taurus Secundus."

Valka realized he was right. She swiped the console, and a scan of the underground showed many natural caves. One seemed inhabited by a host of living creatures moving around. "What are these? It looks like they have tails and wings."

"Demons." Konrad paced nervously, clenching and unclenching his fists. "Our angels fought them before. Nasty little bastards."

Sultan growled in his sleep, as if feeling the tension.

Valka's heart skipped a beat. In her long career as a Valkyrie, she'd never fought demons. She set the scanner to greater depths and another structure emerged on the screen, below the caves, definitely artificial, in the shape of a five-pointed star, with a pulsing beam at its center.

She enhanced the picture on the screen. "Found it. But it's too deep in the rock to destroy it from space, and it's too small of a temple to materialize the ship inside it. Good news is, there is breathable air in that cave."

"We'll have to destroy that pillar from up close, leave the ship in orbit and materialize ourselves inside the temple." Konrad's gaze seemed far away. "Without the ship's big guns, it's extremely dangerous."

"Just the two of us, with no protection, against an army of demons?" Valka realized it could be a suicide mission, but it might be the only way to help their universe... and others. She sighed. "I've lived for millennia. Maybe this is the perfect way to end my life... in a glorious battle."

"Not necessarily." Konrad slicked back his short hair. "We have several NK hand weapons."

Valka scoffed. "Speak for yourself. I can't fire those. I tried."

"From what I know about demons in the angel archives, they can be killed with traditional blasters, and your dragon-fang blade should work, too."

"At least that's something." Valka checked the blasters in her belt. "But how do we destroy that Dark Light?"

Konrad walked to the rack and selected two glowing NK blasters. "With determination, nothing is impossible. We can do this."

Valka resented the military lingo. "Of course, you would say that." She hid her apprehension behind a nervous laugh. "You may be an angel now, but you are still the perfect general, following the rules, and rousing the troops before battle – even if you know they are all going to die."

Konrad shook his head. "Sorry. I can't help it."

The tiger lying on the deck stretched, then rose and yawned, baring sharp teeth and long fangs. *"Sultan fight."*

"Thanks, Sweetheart. We can use your help." Valka scratched the furry head. "I would never go into battle without you."

"Sultan kill nasty critter." The big cat purred, confident in his abilities.

"Are hand weapons strong enough to destroy that pillar of Dark Light, though?" Valka couldn't imagine doing it without a big gun. "What if we dismount one large cannon from the hull and use it to destroy that pillar of Dark Energy?"

"It might work. There are space suits and gravity boots onboard. I've done this kind of work before as a soldier."

Valka could think of many things that could go wrong, but she closed her mind to these thoughts. "Then how do we use it?"

"I can set the big NK gun on the floor of the cave to discharge a constant beam on its own, and the three of us can protect it while it does its work." Konrad's shoulders sagged. "What happens to us after that is in the hands of the Formless One."

"May the spirit of Odin protect us." But if it didn't, at least Valka would have a glorious death, perfect for a Valkyrie.

* * *

Valka rematerialized inside the temple of the Dark Light, in stealth mode, flying on Sultan. Despite the darkness, by the faint glow of torches, she could make out the temple's star shape and high walls covered with hieroglyphics and strange writing, punctuated with horrible scenes of blood sacrifices. She shuddered at the sight.

She couldn't see Konrad who used his own stealth abilities. He was supposed to set the heavy NK gun on the temple floor.

The rush of energy inside the dark pillar at the center of the star-shaped temple vibrated throughout the entire cave, like a freight train speeding through a tunnel. It seemed as if that energy swallowed all light, including the glow of the temple torches. The place smelled of sulfur and brimstone.

All around, the air stirred with a flurry of dark wings. The demons seemed to fly around in panic. They must have detected the intrusion despite the stealth cloaks. Helshades!

The grimacing black creatures had red eyes, long fangs, black fur, and leathery wings, like giant bats, with long grasping tails. They also had arms and legs with gripping fingers and deadly claws. Valka shuddered. Nasty indeed.

"Sultan not like critter." The tiger sounded angry in her head.

Since she couldn't see Konrad, Valka spoke in his mind. *"General, are you okay?"*

"I'm fine. I'm on the floor, setting up the big gun to face the black pillar of energy. Upon my order, it will discharge non-stop on its target." Konrad emitted a mental sigh. *"When it starts, the demons will see its light and attack. Be ready in three, two, One!"*

On the floor below, despite the stealth cloak, the invisible weapon's discharge emitted a bright beam of energy that even the dark pillar couldn't extinguish. The demons who rushed to kill the blue beam of light screamed as it burned them to ashes.

But Valka couldn't let them get to the weapon itself. She jumped off the tiger and landed on the stone floor. "Sultan, kill!"

The tiger flew into the demons' path and shredded their furry bodies, crushing their heads in his powerful jaws. Valka fired her blasters, but even with big holes in their wings, the demons kept attacking.

Then a new vibration flared throughout the temple. Valka's stealth cloak sputtered and died. She could also see Konrad and the cannon, now visible to all. Helshades! Fortunately, the new vibration did not disable the big gun that kept firing blue light at the dark pillar.

Now, the black pillar showed faint signs of weakening... as if the superficial layer of the dark energy beam started flaking... but at this rate, destroying it could take a long time.

Now the demons attacked with unprecedented rage. Their gnarling faces drooled acid that burned holes in the stone, and they screamed at their enemies. Valka repelled them with blaster shots, also throwing blades at their faces, and slicing wings with her sword when they ventured too close.

She could see Konrad hovering above her, firing his special hand weapons. Each blue flare reduced the creatures to ashes in one shot... more efficient than Valka's blasters and blades.

Then one demon grabbed Konrad by the back of the neck, holding his wings, and aimed to throw him into the pillar of Dark Light.

Valka's heart almost stopped. She glanced up at the tiger. "Sultan, dive!"

The tiger dove low enough for Valka to jump on his back. As they flew back up, she sliced the demon's head from its neck in one clean sweep of her dragon-fang sword. The creature lost its grip on Konrad then fell in a swirl like an autumn leaf.

"Thanks." Konrad flapped his wings again and shot three more demons, but they kept coming in waves.

Valka saw no end to the fight. "I don't know how long we can keep them at bay."

Konrad smiled as if he enjoyed the battle. "Let's just hope they don't all attack all at once!"

The demons must have understood Konrad's remark, because they did just that. What now?

Valka summoned a bubble shield that kept the beasties at bay, although some still tried to penetrate it, even as they burned their wings on it. Then she made it explode, stunning the demons, who fluttered toward the ground while Konrad shot them with his special blasters.

Konrad chuckled. "Nice move."

But soon the surviving creatures recovered, and more surged from all directions to join the attack.

Under the relentless charge, Valka started to feel the strain. Konrad also seemed slower to fire. As for Sultan, he still flew despite acid drips on his wings, and snapped at the furry creatures, mauling and cracking bone with his jaws.

Wave after wave of black demons unleashed upon them. Still, the three warriors stood their ground, protecting the angel weapon firing at the dark beam.

As long as they could hold, the weapon would keep firing. That's all that mattered. As the beam of dark energy slowly peeled off and thinned, it lost its ability to absorb the light. It was weakening. Even the roaring energy rushing through the beam had diminished to a whine.

It seemed the demons were weakening, too. They grew more frantic, even throwing themselves in the path of Konrad and Valka's weapons fire. In a desperate attempt to get to the intruders? Or as a sacrifice?

Neither. Valka had seen this before. Better throw yourself on the enemy's sword and die in the glory of battle, than survive a defeat. Suicide, however, was not brave but cowardly, and such warriors would never reach the halls of Valhalla. In Valka's opinion, these demons were cowards.

Finding renewed strength in the enemy's desperation, Valka fired her phaser and slashed and cut, and stunned more creatures for Sultan to maul, while Konrad vaporized his fair share.

But a new wave of fresh creatures emerged from the far corners of the temple, as if the walls were giving birth to new abominations. As they attacked, the whine of the dark beam ceased, and the bright light from the angel cannon filled the space.

The hundreds of newly arrived demons screamed in terror as they shaded their eyes. Then they fell to the floor and twisted as if in horrible pain.

Konrad stopped firing. "I think they can't stand the light."

"That makes sense." Valka glanced around. So many demons littered the floor, dead or dying. "I think we've won."

On the floor, the cannon grew brighter. The energy inside it accelerated, vibrating dangerously fast.

Konrad glanced at it and gasped. "That cannon is about to blow. We have to leave. Now!"

The clickety sound of crumbling stone echoed all around. Dust and gravel dropped from the high vaults.

"Meet you on the ship." Valka patted Sultan. "Let's go, Sweetheart. We need to patch you up."

Sultan growled his assent, and Valka dematerialized with the tiger.

As she rematerialized aboard the *Sweet Freedom*, Konrad was in the control room, returning his NK blasters to the rack. Then he glanced up at the data wall. "The cannons on the hull no longer detect the dark energy signature."

Valka's heart beat like a war drum. "We did it! We destroyed the pillar of Dark Light!"

"Yes, we did." Did he smile? He did.

Sultan sat up on the deck, and Valka examined his spread wings.

"Look at this!" She caressed the white feathers. Black burns marked the spots where acid from the demons' mouths had dripped and charred the skin underneath.

The tiger startled. *"Ouchy!"*

Konrad came and knelt on the deck to check the wounds. "Let me help."

Their hands touched as they caressed the wing, and Valka had a quiver of pure delight. She gazed into Konrad's clear eyes, and he stared right back at her.

"What about your wings?" Valka could see burn marks on his, too.

"They'll heal quickly on their own." Konrad frowned. "What about you?"

"Scratches and bruises." She might have enjoyed a healing session with him, but Valkyries never showed weakness, even in pretense. "Nothing serious."

"Good." Konrad lifted his hand above the tiger. "Sultan? May I touch you to help you feel better?"

The tiger moaned. *"Make Sultan better."*

Konrad applied both hands on the tiger's wings and closed his eyes. Bright blue light surged from his hands. For a few seconds, the entire deck glowed brighter. Even Sultan seemed to glow from the inside.

When Konrad opened his eyes, he smiled.

Sultan licked his face. *"Thank you, angel Konrad."*

"Whoa! You made a big impression." Valka caressed Sultan's healed wings and rejoiced. "I'm impressed, too. There are no marks left anywhere."

The big cat shook himself and retracted his wings. *"Sultan like Angel Konrad."*

Konrad ventured a hand, and Sultan leaned his big head into it for a scratch.

"I think you made a new friend." Glad the tiger warmed up to Konrad, Valka rose and went to the console.

Konrad patted the tiger's head then pushed to his feet. "I think we'll get along fine."

Something on the wall of monitors caught Valka's attention. "Look!"

Konrad joined her and they watched as the fiery planetoid exploded and expanded into a fireball, like a small sun.

Valka could see fast flying debris coming at them. "Shields up!"

Flying boulders knocked the ship and destabilized it. Valka grabbed at the console for support. Smaller debris burned on the shields.

The computer beeped. "No damage recorded."

Valka breathed easier. She pointed to a side monitor. "The deep scans show no remaining artificial structure, not even a deep cave."

"The entire planetoid must have collapsed on itself when the cannon exploded. All that's left is a giant ball of incandescent lava, inside and out." Konrad sounded satisfied.

"Purified by fire." Valka liked that notion. "Mission accomplished."

"Unfortunately, it will not kill Nyxifer, but it will definitely take away a great deal of his power." Konrad sounded proud of their victory.

"I hope so." Valka turned to Konrad hands on her hips. "So, what do we do now?"

"What, indeed?" Konrad flashed a mysterious smile. "I think we should make the most of it. Consider this an opportunity to make this universe our home."

"Our home?" Valka stared into his deep blue eyes. "What do you mean?" She knew exactly what he meant but wasn't ready for it... she may never be.

"We need a quiet place to recoup and heal our wounds and enjoy each other's company... maybe on a warm beach." He stroked a few keys on the console.

"Do you think a vacation is the best idea when our universe is facing enslavement by a red devil?" Valka hoped to avoid the real discussion of intimacy by invoking duty.

"There is nothing more we can do from here." Konrad swiped the console. "Computer, scan this quadrant for a hospitable planet where we could rest and recuperate from our brush with the Dark Light."

"Aye, aye, Captain." The computer beeped. "Searching..."

"Shouldn't we be looking for a way back home? The locals may be able to help us." Valka was running out of excuses.

"Finding our way back home could take a lifetime. Right now, we need to recharge our batteries." Konrad straightened his tall frame. He was truly handsome. "Maybe, we should get used to the idea that this universe could become our new forever home. And we should find our place in it... especially since we are both long-lived."

"This sounds like giving up, and it feels like treason." Now that she was given a logical reason to start afresh, to let go of the past and the guilt attached to it, Valka still dreaded the consequences.

"Why are you resisting the idea? This could be our chance to start over, to have a happy life." Konrad caressed her hand. "I think we deserve it. What are you afraid of?"

"Nothing." A sweet shudder shook Valka from head to toe. She so enjoyed his warm contact. Then a seed of hope sprouted in her mind. "Computer, is there an Asgardian world in this universe?"

Konrad raised his brow. "Now you are thinking."

The computer beeped. "Searching... Searching. This information is not readily available. The data is tangled in layers of clouds and misdirection. It will take time to gather it."

"Keep trying. Asgard was always hard to find, and even more difficult to get to." Valka wondered if Ragnarök had happened here as well... maybe it hadn't.

The computer beeped again. "In the meantime, there is a suitable planet for recuperation. Details and coordinates are being displayed on the monitors."

Konrad smiled at Valka. "Let's check out that planet and enjoy some R&R."

"Since when are you the happy-go-lucky, relaxed type, General?" She'd noticed the same attitude on Azura.

"That's what soldiers do after a victorious battle, or when there is no training or mission to be fought."

Images of a green planet with sand beaches and blue oceans scrolled on the wall monitors. It looked warm and welcoming. Valka realized she could use some rest. "I'm sure Sultan would enjoy running wild."

The tiger's round ears pivoted. *"Sultan hunt blue rabbit?"*

"I'm sure there is small prey to hunt there, Sweetheart." Valka petted the big cat.

Although they were trapped in this universe together with no way home, she still wasn't sure how she felt about letting herself fall in love. It always spelled disaster of galactic proportions for the Valkyries in the past. Even the great Freya could not escape that curse.

Chapter Fourteen

Konrad walked down the belly ramp of the *Sweet Freedom* onto the sandy beach, enjoying the soft evening breeze, the sound of the waves, and the golden glow of the setting sun in a purple sky. He deposited the supplies from the ship on the flat stone covered with a towel, next to the red and yellow fruit he'd harvested from the trees lining the shore.

Then he dug a firepit in the sand, and arranged the driftwood he'd collected earlier, ready to be lit. His experience in the military was coming handy. For seats, he dragged two flat stones from the edge of the beach and placed them on each side of the improvised table. He'd also brought blankets, in case Valka wanted to spend the night under the stars.

The computer had chosen well. The scanners detected no large predators on their deserted island. In the trees, and flying overhead, birds sang, celebrating the end of the day. The red sun slowly sank toward the ocean, and he smelled salt on the sea-breeze.

Konrad sat on one of the smooth rocks, eased his sword to the side, and shaded his eyes against the low sun to watch Valka playing in the waves with Sultan.

Strange couple. They seemed to understand each other... as if she poured all her affections on the cat. She even called him Sweetheart. Did she dislike people? Was she afraid of them? Not likely. She didn't scare easily. Maybe she didn't trust them.

But Konrad remembered her reaction to his touch, back in the crystal cave. And once or twice, when they'd gazed into each other's eyes, the energy that flowed between them was that of a strong mutual attraction. Could he be wrong about that?

Or maybe Valkyries preferred women, like Captain Graziella, who was an Amazon from Skeera before becoming an angel. But Konrad had learned from the Akashic records that deep attraction crossed all boundaries. It transcended gender, race, age, or even species, and often originated in experiences from past lives.

As he watched Valka and Sultan venture into deeper waters, Konrad realized she had left her weapons belt and her boots on the beach, but she still wore her armor, in the water, when there was no danger of attack. Very odd behavior indeed.

Now that there were no more military duties, no more battles to fight, Konrad dared to hope for a different life... a life of peace and harmony... maybe a chance at happiness and freedom from duty... something he'd never known.

When Valka emerged from the water, she flipped her flaxen braids like an Ondine, water running down the amber skin of her shoulders, arms, and legs. The setting sun accentuated her lovely curves. Konrad had never seen anything more beautiful.

Her smile lit up her peridot green eyes. "The water feels wonderful and invigorating. You should try it."

"Maybe later." Raised and trained on spaceships and space stations, Konrad wasn't much of a water creature... although, he enjoyed gazing at the sea.

She sat on the opposite flat rock, untied her flaxen braids, shook her head, then proceeded to loosen and unravel them one at a time. Did she have any idea how sensual her movements were?

"I better light the fire. The nights tend to be cool with the evening breeze." Konrad took his eyes off her with reluctance, not sure whether or not she would welcome his attention.

He searched for the lighter on his utility belt and found it. Then the flames rose, bringing light and warmth. He welcomed the distraction.

She chuckled. "You know I can read your mind, right?"

Was she testing his self-control? "But I can't read yours, so tell me. Do you think we have a future, a chance at a life together? A place in this universe?"

"Maybe." She picked up a fruit and bit into it, juice dripping from her lush lips.

"You keep sending me mixed messages. Sometimes you seem attracted to me, and other times you feel like ice. Why? If you know how I feel about you, you know you can trust me."

"I know." She licked the juice from her lips. "But I never told you my story."

"It seems we have lots of time, now." Konrad rejoiced at the prospect. He wanted to understand her. "I very much wish to hear it."

* * *

Valka considered Konrad's honest face by the dancing light of the flames, and something inside her melted. She started to understand why she liked him so much.

She took a deep breath. "Very long ago, shortly after Odin gifted me with this armor and made me a Valkyrie, I met a handsome man, pure of heart... a mortal. We fell madly in love, but Odin didn't approve of our union. So, we eloped."

She could feel the weight of Konrad's attention on her.

She smiled to lighten the mood. "I left Asgard to be with him on his home planet, with his people. They welcomed me with open arms. I laid down my armor for him, and we were happy for a time. When he died, as mortals do, I retrieved my armor and went to see my mother."

"On Asgard?" He was listening.

"No. On Zephyr. My father was a noble from Asgard, but my mother was a Zephyrian mind reader." Valka closed her eyes briefly, realizing that mixed relationships were often doomed from the start. "On Zephyr, I discovered the planet had been purged of mind-readers, and my mother had been murdered in the latest witch hunt."

"I'm so sorry. Zephyrians have been hunted for millennia because of their gifts." So much compassion in his blue eyes. "In my youth, the GTA leaders trembled at the mention of natural mind readers."

"Then I learned Asgard was no more." Valka swallowed the lump in her throat. "While I enjoyed the company of the man I loved, the entire planet was destroyed according to the prophecy of Ragnarök."

"It's not your fault." His voice caressed her like a warm breeze. "Had you been on Asgard, your mother would still have died, Asgard would have been destroyed... and you would have perished in battle."

"But I missed the most glorious death of all." Valka could never forgive herself for that.

"Death is not glorious." His voice hardened. "It's part of the cycle of life, like birth. And the spirit and soul keep learning over many reincarnations... until we learn all the lessons needed to join the pure energy of the Formless One... and contribute to life on higher levels of existence."

"I can see that, now." Valka felt lighter for unburdening her soul. "But at the time, riddled with guilt, I diligently collected and preserved fragments of Asgardian crystal and bound them together into a large asteroid... now a small planetoid... in an attempt to preserve the magic of Asgard."

He raised his brow. "So, that's what you did with the wealth you amassed chasing and arresting criminals for millennia."

"I hoped if I gathered enough fragments, the crystal might grow together again into a small planet and recreate Asgard... but it could take eons." She stared at the fire. She could almost see her dream realized in the dancing flames. "It was working, too... My small planetoid presents all the properties of Asgard... although not as strong."

Konrad frowned. "But all the Asgardians are dead. Odin is dead."

"There might still be a few isolated beings with Asgardian blood wandering about the universe... like me." As she said it, she realized she'd never met any in her long and lonely existence.

"In any case, that universe doesn't concern us anymore." He reached and gently pushed back a strand of her of her thick, flaxen hair. "We did everything we could to help it. Now, we must learn to live in this one."

Her heart melted at his tender touch. "There is another thing I wanted to tell you." She still wasn't sure, but she trusted him. "After losing everything I loved, while I was being selfish, I swore never again to be distracted from duty by the lure of love."

He shook his head. "Valka, you have punished yourself enough. There is no need to continue this trend here. You are now free of this self-inflicted burden."

"Let me finish." She laid a hand on his knee, sensing his desire. "When I met you, you were everything I wanted to avoid... you reminded me so much of my lost love, that it scared me. But as you said before, there is an attraction between us. And I don't believe in coincidences. Shortly after we met, I had a vision of you with another face... the face of the only man I had ever loved."

His blue stare never wavered.

She wanted him to know everything. "Close your eyes. Let me share this memory with you."

Konrad closed his eyes, and Valka took herself back to a happy time. A simple farm life full of love and hard, honest work, in harmony with nature, changing with the seasons... with horses and cattle, a large community of friends and relatives, celebrating life's every occasion with food, and drink, and songs.

And always at her side, the man she loved, loving her back. The experience was so intense, warm tears rolled down her face. She could now relive the love they had without sadness. That man was here again, and he still loved her, and he wanted a long lifetime with her.

* * *

Konrad came back from Valka's memory shaken, unable to hide his surprise. Yet, deep inside, it rang true. His angel nature could recognize the truth.

Tonight, in this idyllic paradise he could almost remember that simple life with her. The kind of life he'd longed for in his dreams as a young man... before the GTA recruited him to make him a supersoldier. "You are saying I am the reincarnation of the mortal you loved long ago?"

"Yes. I believe you are. But, after our first meeting, you only reminded me of the worst mistake of my entire life. That's why I was so nasty to you. I couldn't let my guard down." She smiled. "But on Azura, I saw another side of you."

He laid his hand on hers. "Valka, we've paid our debt to our universe. There is no more duty, no more rules, no more guilt. It's just you and me, alone in this strange universe for as long as we live."

"It sounds like a dream... feels like a dream, too. None of this seems real."

"Love with no tragic consequences... think about it." Konrad caressed her crystal pendant. "And when we die, in a few thousand cycles, we can bury our crystals on a virgin planet. Over time, they will grow to form a new Azura, generating new angels to protect this universe."

"It sounds so perfect." The ray of hope in her green eyes lit up the beach.

"We can make it happen, you and me." Konrad firmly believed it.

She chuckled. "But there is no such thing as perfection."

He trailed the back of his hand on her bare arm. "I only have to look at you to believe."

Her gaze fixed on him. She slowly pulled the shoulder strap of her armor, and it snapped open. "I haven't removed this armor since he died."

"But he lives in me, and I am very much alive." Konrad caressed the strong fibers of the woven armor... so light and yet so strong. "What is it made of?"

"Asgardian crystal fiber." She caressed his fingers sending tendrils of energy coursing through his body. "Impenetrable to blades or weapon's fire. It's also what gives me my powers. Without it, I revert to a regular Asgardian."

"You lose your powers when you remove it?" Konrad only now realized the depth of her sacrifice. "It's okay. You are safe with me." The crystal at his throat pulsed softly. "My angel powers are intact, and I will protect you if anything happens."

"Good. Because Valkyries are immune to your Blue Crystal transformation. That's why I can never become an angel." She smiled and snapped open the other shoulder strap. "I trust you."

Then she rose and let her armor fall to the sand, revealing her gorgeous body in all its glory. By the light of the driftwood fire, her long amber legs glistened below generous hips, and her Blue Crystal pendant rested between firm breasts... a warrior's body devoid of scars. How rare among non-angels!

Konrad rose to meet her and relished their intimate embrace, like a soothing balm, on an ancient wound that had never healed. Their lips met softly. Her mouth tasted sweet. And for the first time in this life, he felt whole.

They sat on the blanket and she pulled off his white boots, then she snapped open his weapons belt and threw it aside on the sand.

She played with the zipper tag at his neck and slid it down, ever so slowly. "Now, let me help you out of this angel uniform..."

* * *

Valka shuddered in her sleep. She was powerless without her armor, and evil targeted her. She could see Nyxifer, the red hermaphrodite, smiling as he ordered his demons.

"Fetch me the Valkyrie's armor. She and her angel destroyed the source of my power, and now, I will steal hers. The power of Asgard, of all the Valkyries, the power of Odin will be mine!"

"No!" Valka flailed and struggled to awaken from the nightmare, but her legs refused to move. This wasn't just a dream. It was real. She opened her eyes. It was still night, but dawn was near. She could see her armor discarded on the sand a short distance away. She must run for it. But her legs refused to obey her. She was paralyzed.

She wormed through the sand, inch by inch, toward her armor. "Konrad!"

Large birds filled the twilight sky... but it wasn't birds... it was a flock of demons. She touched her crystal pendant and called again. "Konrad, I need your help! Now!"

* * *

Inside the *Sweet Freedom*, a few yards from their picnic site, Konrad whistled as he shaved, then he froze, grabbed his boots and a fresh uniform. Valka was in danger!

He snatched his weapons belt and two NK guns from the rack, then he deployed his wings and dematerialized.

He rematerialized in midair, above the spot where he'd left Valka and saw her desperately crawling toward her armor. High above it, in the dark sky, a flock of demons like those they'd fought in the temple prepared to dive.

"They want my armor for Nyxifer!" The desperate voice came from Valka below him. She had no powers, and some demonic force was paralyzing her.

His heart sank to see her like this, nude and helpless, haggard, long flaxen hair in disarray, exposed to serious injury. But he couldn't go to her now. He must fight the demons to protect her and the armor at any cost.

The tiger flew out of the green vegetation and rose into the midst of demons, attacking with fangs and claws. *"Sultan kill."*

Konrad thought of snatching the armor, but it would only impede him. There were too many demons, and they would never give up. He would have to kill them all.

He hovered above Valka and the armor, facing the attacking demons, then aimed and shot blue beams at the flock, careful to avoid Sultan in their midst. The horrible creatures screamed and vanished when shot. Those Sultan killed or wounded floundered into the waves or thrashed on the sand, too close to Valka for Konrad's taste.

Now, acid drool dripped on the beach, searing the sand. A few drips burned through his wings and his white uniform. He smelled brimstone.

Then another solution came to mind. He snatched the armor, surprised by its feather weight, and dropped it on Valka. If it restored her powers, she would be immune to the demonic spell that paralyzed her, and be able to fight at his side.

But she still struggled on the sand, paralyzed. He would have to help her into her armor.

"Sultan, we need your protection." Konrad landed at Valka's side, spreading his wings to protect her.

"Sultan help." The tiger descended overhead and shielded Konrad and Valka under his majestic wings as well.

Konrad propped Valka to a sitting position, raised her arms, then dropped the armor above her head and closed the shoulder snaps. The armor automatically set into place and shrank to fit Valka perfectly. Magic indeed.

Valka smiled at him and her peridot green eyes shone with radiance. "Good call."

He picked up her weapons belt and handed it to her. "Glad you are back. Now we have to finish the job."

She rose to her feet, clipped the belt, grabbed and shook her boots before donning them, then drew her blaster. "The sky is paling in the east... and they hate the light."

"I remember." Konrad rejoiced at seeing her with full powers again. Hope filled his heart as he aimed at the flocking demons with two blasters.

He fought with Valka at his side, making progress. The demon flock was thinning. Konrad hoped there wouldn't be another wave after this one.

But when the sun bubbled peeking from the low hills on the horizon, the night dissipated. The demons also realized Valka was wearing her armor and they could not win. They screamed and whimpered, then retreated from the light over the ocean, as fast as their wings could carry them. The demons lagging behind dematerialized into dust under the morning rays.

The tiger landed on the sand and shook his wings. *"Sultan win."*

"Yes, big boy. We won." Konrad wouldn't let the cat take all the credit. "Now, let me heal your wounds."

Chapter Fifteen

Aboard the *Sweet Freedom,* resting like a giant bird on their deserted beach, Valka adjusted her armor's straps then started braiding her wild hair, as she scrutinized the maps of their planet on the control room viewers. She felt safer wearing her armor and may never want to remove it again.

The demons' attack had shaken her. The bodies left behind had disintegrated under the direct sun, leaving the beach pristine... but they might return at night.

The hull cameras on the side viewers showed Konrad jogging on the long ribbon of sand, and Sultan frolicking in the waves. Her heart went out to Konrad ... but no place would be safe for them... as long as Nyxifer existed.

The computer beeped. "New information about the Asgard of this universe has been found, Captain."

Valka's heart beat faster. She tied her braids in a top knot. "Do tell."

"The realm still exists, but after Ragnarök failed to destroy it, Asgard went into hiding and remains invisible and inaccessible." The neutral computer voice didn't match the tremendous news.

"But the planet still exists, right?" Hope bubbled inside Valka's chest.

"Affirmative, Captain."

Valka exulted. If the planet existed, its power could be tapped. "Is Odin still alive? Are the Valkyries alive?"

"Unknown." The computer beeped. "That information is not available."

Konrad materialized inside the control room, gorgeous in white jogging pants and tee, and carrying yellow and red fruit in a half shell the size of a large platter. He'd never looked more radiant. "What did I miss?"

Valka's heart fluttered at his mere presence... but she couldn't help blurting her excitement at the news. "Asgard still exists in this universe!"

"Really?" He frowned. "So, you want to go live on Asgard?" His tone remained suspiciously neutral.

"I wish we could. We would be protected there. But Asgard is in hiding and no one can reach it... not even me." Valka realized it might be a good thing. "Besides, if there is another Valka on Asgard, I don't want to face her and tell her all the mistakes I made."

"So..." He set the fruit on the console in front of Valka, his body stiff, his countenance guarded. "What does that mean for us?"

She'd expected more enthusiasm from him. "It means, we can tap Asgard's power to get home."

"Home?" He leaned on the console and crossed his arms. Why wasn't he jumping with joy at the idea? "To our universe?"

"Yes." Valka hid her disappointment at his cool reaction. "Asgard mastered portal technology long ago. They built bridges to travel through space, and between universes."

"How would that work, exactly?" Why wasn't he thrilled about this?

Valka refused to let him steal her happiness. She must convince him. "Through my armor, I can access Asgard's power, and link it to the small planetoid of Asgardian crystal I collected in our universe."

"Sounds risky. It may not work. We could end up in a worse place." Was he skeptical or unwilling?

"It will work." How could she get through to him? "My armor can create a bridge between the two universes."

"Why are you so eager to go back?" Konrad's shoulders sagged. "We weakened Nyxifer, the angels don't need us anymore. Soon, they will kill him, and the demons will stop attacking us."

"Come on." Valka didn't buy his excuses. "The faster we kill that evil monster, the safer we'll be. We can contribute a lot. We know the weapons work and can be improved upon, and we can help them kill that evil monster."

"Since when does a Valkyrie care about the fate of angels?" He gazed at her with so much sadness in his deep blue eyes. "I thought we'd found something special here."

"We did." Could finding love change a man that much? "And why is the stern general in love with rules and duty resisting this opportunity to go back home and serve?"

Konrad rubbed his chin. "I was kind of looking forward to a peaceful existence with you, in this private paradise... I never had that before."

"Actually, we did, in your previous life, and it was wonderful." Valka realized she still wanted that peaceful existence with Konrad, but she didn't deserve it. Not yet. "I lost my world in that bargain, long ago. I was selfish, and I had to live with the guilt. Now that I found you again, I want to do things right."

"There is no reason to feel guilty. We did our part. We could be happy here." His side glance gleamed with promise. "Isn't our love worthy to explore?"

"Of course it is..." She shook her head to resist the temptation. "But believe me, millennia with just each-other on a virgin planet, with no higher duty, no children, no community, no goal, no purpose? Within a month, we would be at each-other's throats."

"When did you become the wise one?" Konrad had a nervous chuckle. "We could find a new purpose in this universe."

Valka stepped up to him and laid both hands on his shoulders. "Don't worry. What we found here can survive the battles to come. If we lose, we die together and find each-other in the next life. If we win and survive, we can start a new life anywhere we choose."

"True." His arms secured her waist and his lips came close for a kiss.

Valka melted in his embrace. He tasted like sweet and spicy fruit. It had been so long since she let herself love. She savored his sweet kiss, never wanting that feeling to end.

When they emerged from the kiss, Konrad smiled and gazed into her eyes. "If that's what it takes to make you happy, let's go home."

* * *

In the sacrificial cave, now deserted and dark, Leader Krow lifted his hood and mask to breathe better. The incense didn't conceal the stench of blood that lingered in the air... so much blood. But it would be worth it when he became the ruler of the entire galaxy. Cycles ago, he'd been respected and feared throughout the quadrant as a GTA leader. People knew his face and he walked proudly in the light.

He'd lost everything when the angels destroyed the GTA. Even his face had suffered ugly and shameful scars... thanks to General Konrad Lagarde. He'd spent many cycles in hiding.

Now, Krow wore a mask and kept to the shadows. But not for long. After the Evil One exterminated all the angels as he promised,

Krow would reclaim his former glory and fame... and take absolute control over the entire galaxy. He would make his enemies pay.

In a red, swirling glow, Nyxifer rose from the stone floor, spinning like a top, then slowed and stood still.

Krow felt naked without his hood and mask as he took a knee on the cold stone before the red hermaphrodite. But he kept his head high and didn't flinch as he held the entity's accusing stare. He wouldn't be intimidated by a foreign devil with an ethereal body.

Nyxifer needed him and the Priory's military might and connections for his personal vendetta against the angels. And Krow would gladly provide it... as long as it served his personal ambition.

"Krow, you failed me." The low voice carried menace. "The angels of this universe possess weapons capable of killing my kind! Why didn't you warn me about this?"

"I didn't know, Exalted Master!" Krow swallowed his pride and bowed. How could he have missed that important detail? But it also meant the red entity could be killed...

Nyxifer glanced with disdain at the many scars visible on Krow's face and shaved skull. "Your body bears the signs of a violent past."

Krow had always been proud of his battle scars... but those ugly, disfiguring ones, inflicted by General Lagarde many cycles ago, still stung his pride... How he wished he'd sacrificed Lagarde when he had him on the altar. But the Valkyrie intervened. "I was a military man before entering the Priory, Exalted Master."

"I see..." Nyxifer hovered a little higher and circled around him without moving... like a statue on a track. "Why didn't you find out about the angels' new weapons? Is your intelligence network lacking? Are you getting soft on your people, and they are getting lazy as a result?"

"Of course not, Exalted Master." Krow hated criticism.

"Because of your ignorance of these new weapons, your general and his Valkyrie were able to destroy my primary source of power in my home universe..." How bold of Nyxifer to admit weakness. "The temple of the Dark Light is no more."

Krow took mental notes. The red devil was getting arrogant and sloppy. "I am sorry, Exalted Master."

"Are you?" The hermaphrodite sounded mad.

Unwillingly, Krow found himself bowing so low that his head touched the cold stone. Damn the red devil and his weird control on human beings. Then Krow's words came unbidden. "What can I do to help you now, Exalted Master?"

The red entity snarled. "Since my demons could not steal the Valkyrie's armor... Only one thing can help me sustain my strength now."

"What is it, Exalted Master? Name it, and I will provide it." Krow hated this imposed groveling... but it wouldn't last forever. A plan was forming in his mind.

"I want a thousand blood sacrifices in my name." Nyxifer straightened and seemed to grow larger. "That should sustain me for a while."

"A thousand?" Krow may not have that many prisoners on hand, but he couldn't refuse. "It will be done, Exalted Master."

"Good." Nyxifer turned as if to leave then froze. "Also, your former general and his Valkyrie might return soon. I want his blood as well."

"It will be my pleasure, Exalted Master. I live to obey your command." That part, Krow would enjoy. "What about the Valkyrie?"

"I have special plans for the Valkyrie." Nyxifer emitted a sinister giggle and vanished.

Krow released a breath of relief and straightened his back. Bowing did not suit him. He was using Nyxifer to augment his power, not the other way around. The red devil grew more demanding. Krow would have to get rid of him while he was weak. But first, he would let angels and demons destroy each other.

Then, with the angels gone and no one to get in his way, Krow could reign supreme in the galaxy.

* * *

"Are you ready?" Sitting in the captain's chair of the *Sweet Freedom*, Valka hesitated. Her hand went to her throat. "I miss your crystal pendant."

Konrad inclined his head and smiled reassuringly. "Don't worry. I'll make you another one. There is plenty of crystal on Azura. This one, buried in our special paradise, will ensure this universe sees the rise of new angels. Even if it's in the far future."

"I know. It's a good thing." She froze, hands on her shoulders, ready to snap open her armor. Removing it had always proved deadly for Valkyries. The incident on the beach only proved it.

"Are you sure you need to remove it?" Konrad's eyes narrowed with concern.

"Yes, I am sure." Valka steeled her resolve. "Because I want to transport us all, along with the ship. If I kept it on, it would only transport me. This is not a simple dematerialization."

Konrad nodded his understanding. "You can do this."

"*Sultan ready.*" The tiger flattened himself on the soft deck.

Fear made Valka tremble. "What if the demons attack again? I will be helpless."

"I'm here for you." Konrad's blue gaze softened. "Besides, demons will not attack in the bright light of day."

"True." Still, Valka's chest filled with dread. She calmed her misgivings and gathered the courage to overcome her fears. She must remain in control. She couldn't lose her armor to the clutches of evil. "Let's do this."

"Where in our universe shall we go?" Konrad sounded so calm.

"In the vicinity of Krow's stronghold. No doubt the angels got my message that Nyxifer was there. They will be assembling for battle."

Valka unsnapped her shoulder straps, lifted the armor from her body, and let it float between her and Konrad, where it rotated slowly in the space. She strapped herself in the captain's chair, then closed her eyes and focused on the familiar Asgardian vibration.

"By the magic of Asgard and the powers of Odin, with the help of Heimdall and Freya, and all the Valkyries, bridge this universe to mine, and take us to the vicinity of Taurus Secundus!"

In a flash, Valka saw Asgard in all its splendor, with its golden towers and walls, and the magic crystal making everything sing with life. For a moment, she was home, and a warm tear rolled down her cheek. Then she met Heimdall's golden eyes, and knew he'd heard her. Did he care that she came from another universe? He didn't seem to mind.

With a whooshing sound, the long rainbow bridge, the Bifrost, threaded through her armor like an arrow through the eye of a needle.

Then the entire ship fell very fast. Valka glanced Sultan gripping the soft deck with his claws, and Konrad grasping the armrests of his seat. Then, the ship spun like a top while falling into a well... and all went black.

* * *

Graziella the Merciful rematerialized the *Blue Phantom* behind the largest moon of Taurus Secundus but kept it in stealth mode. All around, she could sense the entire Azuran fleet getting into attack formation. The Great Lady of Azura had told them to wait for a signal, so she waited, feeling the same tension in the minds of all the angel fleet captains.

A strange phenomenon made her focus on a small slice of dark space. There, close enough for the eye to see, a rift in space revealed a bright light, and in that light a small vessel appeared. Was that the sign the Great Lady mentioned?

"Foreign vessel, identify yourself!" As no answer followed, Graziella asked an Android angel on the bridge. "Scan the vessel… but be careful not to reveal our presence."

The Android purred and its silver body emitted a blue glow. "The vessel is Azuran… a small yacht, the *Sweet Freedom*… vanished from Azura's shipyard yesterday."

"Why aren't they in stealth mode?" Graziella guessed it must be the vessel Valka borrowed to go rescue the general. "Anyone onboard?"

"Two faint life-signs, Captain. One is an angel. They are not moving and must be unconscious."

Graziella hoped the angel was General Konrad Lagarde. She needed her first mate for the great battle. "Cloak the *Sweet Freedom* and bring it to the *Blue Phantom* immediately."

"Aye, aye, Captain." The android glowed brighter as it focused its synthetic mind on the task.

* * *

Konrad came to on the soft deck of the *Sweet Freedom* and rubbed his forehead. Somehow, his seatbelt had broken and he had been thrown to the deck. Through blurred vision he could see Sultan, like a tiger-striped blob, retching in a corner.

"Valka? Where are you?" As his vision cleared, he realized she was nowhere in sight. Her armor, too, was gone. "Valka!"

Sultan emitted a forlorn roar. *"Valka not here."*

"Computer, where are we?" Konrad dreaded the answer. "What happened? Where is Valka?"

The onboard computer beeped. "It seems we are back in our universe of origin, Captain."

"What about Valka? Where is she?" He sounded desperate to his own ears.

"Valka's vibration is not detected in the vicinity, Captain." The computer didn't care at all.

"Where could she be? Suggest an explanation." Konrad refused to consider the worst.

The computer beeped. "She might have remained behind in the other universe, Captain."

"Impossible. She was with me on this ship as we entered the rainbow bridge. Try again. She has to be here." Konrad refused to believe she'd vanished in the rift between universes.

"Scanning... scanning..."

If only she'd been wearing her crystal pendant. But since they'd left it behind, Konrad had no way of locating her.

The computer beeped. "Captain, I detect a large Azuran fleet in the vicinity. They are in stealth mode. It seems a tractor-beam is pulling the *Sweet Freedom* toward the *Blue Phantom*."

"Sultan feel many angel." The tiger shook his head. *"Sultan want Valka."*

Konrad scratched the tiger's head. "Me too, big boy. Me too."

The presence of the fleet was no consolation. Hot anger rose in Konrad's throat. They shouldn't have returned. They were happy and safe in their beach paradise. They should have remained there.

Now, he suspected Valka was in mortal danger, and if Nyxifer somehow got hold of her armor, their return would make things worse for the people of his universe.

* * *

Konrad walked onto the Command Deck of the *Blue Phantom*, his mind struggling with Valka's disappearance.

Graziella the Merciful smiled as she saw him. "General, I'm glad to see you alive. Where have you been? We could use your expertise."

"Thanks, Captain. Valka saved me from being sacrificed to evil, then Nyxifer propelled us into his own universe." Konrad wanted to be done with the formal report. Valka was in danger.

"Another universe?" Graziella's face betrayed her emotions as she read Konrad's mind. "Do tell."

"We were able to return, but now Valka is missing." Konrad welcomed Graziella's gentle intrusion in his mind. "I suspect Nyxifer snatched her, somehow."

"I am so sorry to hear that Valka is missing, General. but right now, we must focus on the battle at hand."

"I understand." Konrad squared his shoulders. "Valka and I destroyed the source of Nyxifer's power in his universe. He should now be weakened..."

"Great. How did you manage to destroy his main power source? Short version." Graziella was reading the details in his mind.

"Our Nyxifer-killing weapons can be adapted to scan and target anyone and any technology coming from his universe." Konrad spoke fast, eager to find and rescue Valka.

"Would that include their special EMP wave weapon?" Graziella sounded hopeful.

"It should. I know how to modify our weapons... and include that technology in our shields, to disrupt their special EMP. You can get the details directly from my mind." There, that should be enough. Konrad needed to find Valka.

"Great. Let's hope it works." Graziella turned to the android. "Read the information from the general's mind and spread it to the entire fleet immediately." She focused on Konrad. "Anything else we should know?"

"Yes." Konrad wanted to be done here. "Although we destroyed his temple and his pillar of Dark Light, if Nyxifer is in possession of Valka's armor, he might be able to use it as an alternate source of power."

"Noted." Captain Graziella straightened. "Now, show us what we need to do."

"Aye, aye, Captain." Konrad closed his eyes and synched his mind with that of the android. The synthetic angel hummed as he transmitted the information to adapt the weapons and shields. All the angels on all the ships in the fleet would receive it instantly.

When Konrad opened his eyes, he stepped closer to Graziella. "We must strike while Nyxifer is weak, before he finds another power source... He sent his demons to steal Valka's armor, the source of her powers. We defeated them, but now he may have succeeded."

"May I read your mind for the full details?" Graziella's gaze never wavered.

Konrad nodded then straightened his tall frame. Many emotions assailed him as Graziella read his mind... especially the memory of the battle with the demons in the underground temple... the destruction of the dark beam... another battle on a beach... and much more... She seemed to understand how much Konrad lost when Valka went missing.

"I'm so sorry, General. Any idea where Valka might be detained?" Captain Graziella the Merciful seemed genuinely concerned. She cared for everyone, even Valka, who wasn't an angel.

"I'd bet it's in that infernal cave where I was imprisoned... they have cuffs that neutralize angel abilities." Konrad shook his head in an attempt to chase away the bad memory.

Graziella touched his arm gently. "I'm sure she is alive, nearby, General."

"I can't let these monsters sacrifice her to their unholy altar." The very thought made Konrad sick to his stomach.

Graziella the Merciful gave him a mental hug. "We will find her, General. I promise."

Konrad certainly hoped so. He didn't want to live his long life without her.

Chapter Sixteen

Valka's shoulders and ribs ached, but she couldn't feel her legs. The smooth floor where she lay felt like glass, and unusually warm against her skin. She twitched her nostrils at a sweet-sour smell then strained her hearing, but she could not place the faraway whine that filled the space with a strange vibration.

A subtle warning raised the small hairs on her back, jolting her awake. As she sat up and looked around, she saw a perfect dome made of shiny green crystal, which was large enough to be a public temple, but was bare and empty. A weak glow emanated from the dome itself, providing an eerie light.

Valka didn't recognize the place. Where was she?

As she looked down, she realized she only wore undergarments. No armor! No weapons. No boots either. She always stashed blades in her boots. Her bare legs felt numb. Metal cuffs with blinking lights restrained her wrists, and her ankles were chained through a metal ring anchored into the crystal floor. She was caged like a dangerous animal. No one in sight.

Then she remembered removing her armor and using it to cross the rainbow bridge. Helshades!

"Konrad! Sultan!" Her voice echoed her desperation across the empty dome. Where were they? Were they safe?

No answer came... only the strange whine pervading the space. So, she focused on the two of them and called them in her mind. *"Konrad, Sultan, are you safe?"*

A jolt from the cuffs made her cry out in pain.

But she couldn't feel the familiar tingle of contact. Did the whine interfere with mind communications? Did the green crystal shield her from the outside world? Or, was it worse? Had she lost all powers? It couldn't be. Even without her Valkyrie's armor, she was still a Zephyrian mind reader.

Then she remembered Konrad mentioning the blinking cuffs had neutralized his angel abilities when he was taken prisoner. By Thor's hammer, Konrad was right. Returning to their universe had been a mistake.

"Odin, please, let it be a bad dream." But she suspected this was not simply a nightmare.

No answer came. She realized with dread that no one could hear her. Not the spirit of Odin, nor those of the Valkyries. She slowed her racing heart. She must not give in to fear. She needed to calm down and think.

She could easily guess who her jailor was. If Nyxifer had somehow snatched her armor, she was at his mercy... and she suspected he had none. But he couldn't tap

the power of the Valkyries without her help–
and she would never give it.

A red glow whirled in front of her. Although she couldn't see Nyxifer, his hovering presence reeked of ill-gained power... the power of blood, built on stolen lives. She attempted to read his mind but came up blank.

With her legs paralyzed, Valka could only sit. She straightened her back. If Nyxifer had studied Asgardian lore, he would try to seduce her into showing him how to use the power of the Valkyries. Valka would refuse. Too many lives depended on her will to prevent Nyxifer from using the armor to boost his abilities.

"So... you are awake..." The disembodied voice echoing through the glassy dome dripped with poisoned honey.

Valka shivered at the very thought of what Nyxifer might do to her. Her heart stumbled in her chest. She refused to play mind games with evil, but given her situation, she may not have a choice. She steeled her resolve. She must not show weakness.

Then the naked hermaphrodite materialized into the reddish glow. Despite the cruel glint in his eyes, some might consider him beautiful... from the symmetrical features of the face, to the gleaming horns and generous breasts, to the muscular body.

Valka struggled to rise, teetering on numb legs like blocks of ice. She managed to stand upright.

"With your armor in my possession, I can control you, Valkyrie." So much satisfaction in the suave voice. "I can make you fall in love with me, and teach me how to use the armor to draw on Odin's powers."

"Never!" But better Valkyries had fallen into that trap in the past... including the great goddess Freya herself. Deprived of their armor, the Valkyries became vulnerable, easy to influence... and Nyxifer knew it. Helshades!

"You cannot win, Valkyrie." Nyxifer drew closer. "No one can find you here. Help is not coming. You have no choice and will surrender."

"We destroyed your pillar of Dark Light." Valka toughened her resolve. "Do with me what you will. I won't tell you the armor's secret, and soon, the angels will kill you."

"I don't think so." So much glee in the handsome red face. "Truth is, the angels can't reach me here."

With awkward feet, no longer numb as ice, but now on pins and needles, Valka somehow managed a narrow combat stance, limited by the short chain between her ankles, cuffed fists ready to strike as one.

"Really? Even now, you won't give up?" Nyxifer scoffed. "What can you possibly do to me in your pitiful state? You are like a newborn kitten threatening a solitary tiger."

Valka took one step forward to strike the red devil, but she ran short of chain. Then some unseen force shoved her down to the floor. Helshades! She struggled to get back on her feet and reached an awkward stance. She couldn't find her balance.

"I admire your efforts, Valkyrie." Nyxifer's voice rang with glee, and his dark eyes matched his cruel smile. He visibly enjoyed her predicament. "But don't feel bad. Even the angels can't touch me... and their new weapons are useless here."

"I don't believe you." If Valka could make him talk, maybe she could discover a weakness, possibly escape, warn the angels. She needed more information. "Where are we, exactly?"

"Don't worry, the angels will never find us." Nyxifer extended his arms and turned to show off the dome. "This is a special chamber, shielded with technology from my universe... undetectable for your angel friends, and unbreachable."

"Unbreachable?" Valka remembered the Temple of the Dark Light inside the alien planetoid. It must have been shielded the same way, but she and Konrad had materialized inside without incident. "Only until it's breached."

The entity's face hardened. "This place is undetectable and perfectly safe. No one knows it even exists."

Valka wondered if evil could fall to vanity. "If it is that safe, there is no harm in telling me where we are."

"Why not?" Nyxifer smiled but his conniving eyes didn't. "We are at the heart of Taurus Secundus... inside the planet's molten core."

"Really?" No wonder it was warm. Valka's hopes sank. "Exceptional technology indeed."

"Thank you." Nyxifer hovered closer, studying her exposed body with open desire. "I could show you more of my talents, if you wish." His voice caressed her. "I have many skills."

"I don't doubt it, but you are wasting your time." Valka wouldn't get intimidated or seduced. "I will never fall under your charms."

"Why not? Without your armor you are not immune..." He gazed deep into her eyes then raised his brow in surprise. "Oh! You are in love with that angel who seduced you on the beach?"

Valka resented that the entity knew that. "It's none of your business."

"All right. I get it." Nyxifer jeered. "But if you let me have the power of the armor, I can save him... make sure he remains safe when I massacre the rest of the angels... then you two can live happily together forever..."

Valka must not be tempted. She must believe the angels could win. The fate of the entire universe was at stake. Besides, the red devil would never keep his word. "I don't trust you."

"That's all right. You will." Nyxifer seemed to grow in size.

Valka stepped back but ran out of chain. The entity came closer and encompassed her with his red glow. She felt strange, as if floating between worlds. Did Nyxifer control her mind? Her head whirled.

She was walking on the beach, naked, Konrad at her side. He caressed her shoulder as he'd done many times last night. Valka felt aroused and confused. She could only remember their love, and nothing else. She couldn't resist Konrad's voice, his magnetism, his enticing angel scent.

He pushed away a strand of her flaxen hair. "I do love rules, but some are meant to be broken. We've done all we could. We deserve happiness. We should stay here and enjoy each-other forever in this tropical paradise."

How could Valka resist his wishes? "Of course, my love, we can stay here forever."

But something pulled at the back of her mind. What was it she couldn't remember? Something was wrong... but what? Something was missing... Sultan.

She scanned the beach. "Sultan!"

No answer in her mind. No tiger emerged from the waves or surged from the greenery at the edge of the beach.

"Who is Sultan?" Konrad's brow furrowed in puzzlement.

Something was definitely wrong.

Valka stepped away from Konrad and shook her head to clear her mind. The tropical surroundings disappeared. She sat in the green crystal dome, chained to the floor, and alone...

* * *

Inside the cave temple on Taurus Secundus, lit by the flames of many torches, heavy smoke rose toward the high vaults. Krow almost gagged on the stench of the thousand sacrifices. Three officiants, on three altar stones, nonstop for five standard hours. So much blood... It mucked the floor and fouled the smell of the incense.

Although Krow usually enjoyed this kind of thing, the mass killings didn't allow for finesse or attention to detail. There was no artistry, no skill, no time to enjoy the prolonged agony of each sacrifice, the slow twist of the knife, or the intense fear in the eyes of the doomed.

The hooded monks, soldiers, and acolytes, assembled to witness the rise of Nyxifer to power, chanted to the frenzied rhythm of the drums. "Hail Nyxifer! Hail Nyxifer!"

Krow's knife arm ached, stiff and sore from so many ritual thrusts of the blade. Nevertheless, he stared into the frightened face of the last sacrifice and plunged the dagger in the man's chest, piercing the rib cage. The scream ended. Blood gushed across the altar stone, thick with the dried offal of the previous kills.

From the corner of his eye, beyond the black mask hiding his identity, Krow watched the Evil Master, standing still in his crimson skin, breasts heaving, eager to claim more blood.

Krow ripped and cut off the last heart and raised it. "Exalted Master, Lord Nyxifer, Bringer of Darkness! Accept this small offering. We are welcoming your reign in this universe."

The naked entity snarled then drooled as he took the heart and opened a wide mouth then swallowed the bloody offering in one gulp. Krow wondered how he could eat flesh and drink blood, since his body wasn't entirely solid. But he looked denser with each sacrifice. Krow would have to get rid of this abomination before he became too strong.

"All hail Nyxifer! All hail Nyxifer!" the monks and acolytes repeated in a trance.

The red entity wiped the blood from his mouth with the back of his wrist, then turned to Krow. "I need more sacrifices," he whispered. "Blood energy is not as strong as my previous power source."

Krow bowed low and whispered back. "But, Exalted Master, we have sacrificed all the prisoners. This was the last one. Didn't the Valkyrie's armor help restore your powers?"

"Not yet. I need more time before I can draw from it." The red hermaphrodite sneered. "To bridge the gap, I need more sacrifices... kill the civilian population... whatever it takes."

"But, Exalted Master, this is a military planet. Civilians are few."

"Then kill your own men, the monks, the acolytes, I don't care. Find me more blood and fast... or else..."

Krow bowed, glad for the mask concealing his displeasure. He willed his voice to be submissive. "It will be done, Exalted Master."

"Make sure of it." The menace in the Master's hushed tone was unmistakable. Then Nyxifer dematerialized, his red glow dissipating in the smoke of the torches.

Krow raised both arms to the high vaults and recited the closing words in a strong voice for everyone to hear. "May the darkness conceal us as we work to become the masters of this universe."

"Hail the darkness! Hail the darkness!" The acolytes and hooded monks answered, then they bowed and slowly filed out of the temple.

Krow brushed bloody chunks off his black robe with a hint of impatience. He opened and closed his fist and shook his aching arm. The whole Nyxifer enterprise wasn't going as planned. The entity promised to rid this universe of angels, but instead, he exhausted Krow's resources, while giving nothing in return.

Krow had still to see the formidable military force the red devil had promised.

At the sound of hurried footsteps, Krow adjusted his hood and his mask over his face and turned to see the captain of the guard rushing toward him gasping for breath.

The guard captain took a knee. "Lord Abbott... a large angel fleet is poised behind the largest moon, just out of striking range... We didn't see them coming... All of a sudden, they showed on our scanners..."

"Of course they came." Great! Now Krow had to fight the angels himself.

"What are your orders, Lord Abbott?"

Krow waved away the guard captain. Fortunately, his fleet was nearby. He touched his neck and spoke. "Admiral!"

His communicator buzzed. "Yes, Lord Abbott."

"The Azurans are here, behind the large moon. Bring the Priory fleet to bear behind them at once, and prepare to deploy the special angel EMP weapon." As Krow raised his head, the guard captain was still kneeling on the stone floor, waiting.

The man bowed low. "What should I do, Lord Abbott?"

"Order the Cyborgs to round up a hundred civilians and bring them here as quickly as possible." That might appease the red devil.

The captain frowned. "Civilians? But Lord Abbott, I'm not sure there are any left."

"There must be some in the compound, servants, cooks, janitors, unworthy lowly military rejects. Be creative. Victory requires more human sacrifices." Krow growled. "Or do you prefer I immolate you on the altar stone?"

"No, Lord Abbott. One hundred will be provided." The man bowed so low his head touched the bloody floor. Then he rose, took a few steps back, eyes down, turned around, and hurried out of the temple.

"Finally, some action." Nyxifer manifested in front of Krow.

Krow bowed. Had the entity ever left? Or had he been spying from the shadows all along?

The red devil scoffed. "Time to show the angels how insignificant they are."

Krow nodded. "You sound sure of yourself, Exalted Master." The moment of truth had come. "So, where is the supernatural military help you promised?"

"Oh, ye of little faith…" Nyxifer's smile looked more like a sneer. "My demonic legions are on their way."

"Legions of demons? At last…" Maybe the angels and demons could kill each other. Then Krow could kill Nyxifer.

The evil Master's red face turned serious. "And these demons thrive on my power. So, if you want victory, you better get me more blood and soon."

"You will have it within the hour, Exalted Master."

As the red devil vanished again, Krow realized it might behoove him to delay the sacrifices, and keep Nyxifer weak, in case he needed to kill him... maybe with one of those new Nyxifer-killing weapons the angels had concocted... the very same his spies had failed to report. The weapons that cost Krow a severe reprimand and destroyed the Exalted Master's original power source.

It might be possible to procure such a weapon in the heat of battle, or after the victory. Better weapons make the spoils of war.

* * *

On the control deck of the *Blue Phantom*, where the captain had assembled the officers, Konrad attempted to contact Valka one more time. *"Beloved, can you hear me? Where are you?"*

No answer, as before. Konrad couldn't stop thinking about Valka. He must believe she was alive, although all his efforts to locate her or the armor had failed.

The evil one must have them both. And since the Dark Light had been destroyed, Nyxifer would do anything to possess the Valkyries' power. Konrad understood now that the power in that armor was much greater than anyone realized. No wonder Nyxifer wanted to possess it.

Konrad closed his eyes, begging for the Formless One to protect Valka. He didn't want to think what Nyxifer might do to her, if he had her in custody.

"They know we are here." The captain stared at the 3D display of the battlefield.

A small enemy fleet was taking positions to protect Taurus Secundus. On a side screen, the progress of the new updates to the Nyxifer-killing weapons, and the anti EMP shields showed ninety-five percent complete.

The trip to Nyxifer's universe had taught Konrad a lot about their shields and weapons. These new adjustments would make the latest angel weapons even more effective. This could make a big difference in the outcome of the final battle.

Captain Graziella the Merciful was also staring at the monitors, with more tension in her handsome face than usual. She rubbed her chin, then nervously raked her short blond hair. "Let's hope these upgraded shields and weapons are effective against theirs."

"They will be." Konrad hoped he wasn't lying.

"I am receiving orders from Fleet Command." The captain closed her eyes and listened, then she issued a mental order for the *Blue Phantom.* *"Deploy the shields."*

An eerie blue cloud enveloped the angel fleet.

As if on cue, the enemy fleet reacted with a slight wave of weapons energy. They were activating their anti-crystal EMP wave. The angels on deck held their breath. So did Konrad. This was the moment of truth. The brand-new updates to the angel shields to resist the EMP had never been tested.

"Brace!" The captain shouted. "Here comes the wave."

On the 3D hologram, a strong luminous surge from the enemy fleet hit the protective shields of all the angel vessels, linked together into an elliptical cloud. The shields flared blue as they absorbed most of the shock. Only a slight bump affected the *Blue Phantom*. But more importantly, all the lights remained on.

"Report!" The captain closed her eyes. When she opened them, she smiled. "The new shields are holding against their special EMP. None of our vessels were neutralized."

The angels on deck cheered.

So did Konrad. "Let's hope the hand weapons are as effective."

Captain Graziella nodded her agreement.

"Captain!" An android angel manifested on the control deck. "A large enemy fleet is gathering behind us!"

Captain Graziella closed her eyes. "Keep feeding the shields!"

Another android materialized on the deck. "Captain, Nyxifer's signature is detected near the sacrificial cave!"

"Good." Captain Graziella straightened her back, closed her eyes as if to confirm her orders then opened them. "Time to execute our attack plan!"

Konrad attempted again to locate Valka, to no avail. He approached Graziella. "Captain, permission to lead a small group to insure Nyxifer doesn't use Valka's armor."

"Take a few androids with you. They won't be influenced by Nyxifer's mind tricks... not with the modifications we just implemented." The captain smiled. "Go, but wait for my signal before manifesting down there. Let us clear the surface first."

"Thank you, Captain." Konrad saluted and walked away.

He hoped he wouldn't be too late. Wherever Nyxifer was, Valka would be close by, and she definitely needed help. Konrad stopped and pushed a lock in the bulkhead. The panel lifted with a whoosh of compressed air.

Behind it, Sultan sat up, round ears pivoting, tail twitching, questions in his eyes. *"Time?"*

"Yes, big boy, it's time. Come on. Let's go find Valka." Konrad would need all the help he could muster. The tiger was brave and deadly in battle... he could also track Valka's scent, and he very much cared for her.

"Sultan find Valka. Sultan save!" The big cat growled as if to steel his resolve.

The two companions hurried toward Bay Five, where the first attack wave of ships and flying androids gathered. Konrad sent a mental message to the android garrison on the *Blue Phantom*. *"Request five androids to meet me in Bay Five for special mission."*

"Order acknowledged, General. Sending you five units now." The synthetic voice in his head denoted no emotion.

Against all odds, hope surged in Konrad's chest. This desperate mission might just work... but could he find Valka before Nyxifer tortured her? Or worse... sacrificed her to his unholy purpose?

Konrad walked faster. By the grace of the Formless One, may he find Valka alive.

Chapter Seventeen

On the Command Deck of the *Blue Phantom*, Graziella the Merciful took a slow breath as her officers gathered around the 3D rendering of the space battlefield. They stared at it with stiff faces and anxious eyes. The android angels, however, remained on the periphery, calm and collected as was their nature.

Closing her eyes, Graziella focused on the other angel captains in the fleet, to receive confirmation of her orders from Fleet Command. In her mind, she saw the captains' faces, some human, some with alien features, or brightly colored skin. The captains listened then nodded. So did she.

Graziella opened her eyes. "Orders confirmed."

The 3D hologram showed the long-range angel weapons linking together, creating a blue sphere of energy around the angel fleet. It also showed the surrounding enemy vessels as they advanced slowly but steadily into weapons range, their hull cannons aimed and ready to strike.

Graziella focused on the count down from Fleet Command in her head. "On my mark... three, two, one, fire!"

From the sphere of lightning trails encompassing the angel fleet, a blue wave surged outward on all sides, scattering and tossing the enemy vessels like corks on an angry sea.

The Priory blockade in front of the planet, and the destroyers behind the angel fleet no longer held their positions. Their warships floated away, topsy turvy, disorganized, unprepared for this kind of attack. Many Priory vessels in close proximity bumped each other violently, causing fiery explosions in space from the escaping oxygen. The gutted enemy ships sparked and oozed a steady flow of people, Cyborgs, and debris.

Graziella rejoiced, and all the angels on the Command Deck cheered... even the androids.

A few enemy destroyers still in working order sped up to meet the advancing angel fleet, but despite their shield-piercing weapons pounding at the blue bubble, the Azuran shields held strong.

Still, Graziella wanted a complete victory. She contacted the other captains in her mind. *"Let's make our shields reflective."*

The other captains nodded agreement. On the display, the blue shields shimmered at a different frequency.

As the remaining Priory destroyers came closer and fired again, their fiery red energy beams bounced off the blue shields. Then the angels blasted their hull cannons, and the enemy destroyers exploded and disintegrated, leaving Taurus Secundus exposed.

With the Priory fleet neutralized, the planet defenses activated their long-range missiles. A flurry of deadly rockets exploded harmlessly on the angel shields like orange fireworks, that spread on the blue surface, like blooming flowers.

Graziella closed her eyes to listen to the orders from Fleet Command in her head, then repeated them for her crew. "Target the planetary shields." She opened her eyes and stared at the 3D hologram. "On my mark... three, two, one, fire!"

A blue wave hit the planetary shields that flashed red, but the barrier only wavered. The shield generators, visible from space, remained intact and protected.

Graziella closed her eyes and called the other angel captains. *"Did we get their shield codes from their downed destroyers?"*

"One of our androids just manifested on one of the wrecks. He's transmitting the codes right now." No emotion in the synthetic mind voice.

"Codes received. Thanks." Graziella opened a channel to her crew through the ship-wide system. "Insert enemy shield codes and target their land cannons, missile launchers, shield generators, and main complex buildings! Fire as they bear!"

A hundred beams of concentrated energy hit the surface, destroying many buildings of the main complex. Fiery explosions riddled the hangars. Towers and fortified positions crumbled. Cannon bunkers and missile silos imploded in clouds of smoke before erupting into flames.

The shield generators exploded and the reddish barrier wavered and died. But the main part of the Priory headquarters lay deep underground, safe from space weapons.

A flurry of small enemy ships on the ground scrambled and took flight, targeting and launching their weapons at the approaching angel fleet. They rained volleys of small projectiles, but those fizzled on the Azuran shields, which remained impenetrable, especially when linked together.

Then the angel fleet fired back with a mighty wave, wiping out all the small fighters as it passed.

Graziella rejoiced, but it seemed too easy. So far, they'd only encountered traditional defenses, nothing outlandish or unexpected. Where was Nyxifer's army? "Landing parties, the coast is clear, but watch out for demonic creatures and boobytraps."

* * *

Konrad materialized in midair inside the sacrificial cave where Nyxifer had been detected, riding Sultan but invisible. The stench of blood was overpowering. The infernal drums, the lugubrious chanting, the smoke and the torchlight gave Konrad a cold shiver at the memory of his near-demise, only less than two days ago on that same altar.

At the center of the wheel-shaped design of the temple floor, an officiant Abbott stood, blade poised, reciting evil verses over the unfortunate wretch chained to the bloody stone. The doomed man hyperventilated and struggled to scream as he stared at the sacrificial blade, his chest rising and falling at an accelerated tempo.

Konrad shuddered as he recognized the unmistakable supersoldier stature of the officiant, the stiff shoulders, and the way the man held his head high... and the hatred in the cruel eyes behind the mask. It was Killer Krow... again. How Konrad wanted to smash his ugly face into the bloody stone.

But there was too much at stake. Valka and Nyxifer must be his priority. Konrad must not reveal himself, not yet. Where was Valka? Where was Nyxifer?

The five android angels on Konrad's team materialized on the periphery of the circular temple, behind the disciples in red hooded robes kneeling in prayer, eyes closed. From the corner of his eyes, Konrad saw the androids disarming and neutralizing the Cyborg soldiers guarding the entrances. Good.

Konrad focused on Valka, trying to locate her with his mind, to no avail. She wasn't in reach. Too far away? Shielded? Or worse? *"Sultan, can you track Valka?"*

The tiger flapped his wings and sniffed the air. *"Valka not here."*

Konrad's heartbeat accelerated. Was she still alive? He must not lose hope.

A nearby explosion, followed by several tremors, rumbled through the cavern like a small earthquake. Stone dust and gravel rained down from the high vaults, probably due to the pounding of the surface by angel weapons. But inside the cave, the drums kept beating, and the ghastly chanting went on, as if these evil worshipers believed the caverns to be indestructible and impenetrable.

Killer Krow's dagger remained poised above the sacrifice as he stared at the high vaults, reciting litanies.

A Cyborg burst through a back entrance. "Intruders!"

More Cyborg and black-armored soldiers rushed into the sanctum. "Angels inside the stronghold!"

The security forces engaged the few android angels inside the temple. The angels flew up and rained blue lightning on the black-clad soldiers. Screams filled the air, replacing the chanting.

The hooded acolytes glanced around with fear on their faces. Several drew red daggers from their belts while others scattered toward the exits. But Nyxifer appeared, floating above the altar like an ethereal red shadow. The fleeing acolytes froze and gasped, then knelt and bowed, head to the stone floor, as if pleading for forgiveness for a capital offense.

Krow sheathed his blade and knelt by the altar, but his head remained high.

The entity made of red smoke looked disapprovingly upon his flock. "Ye of little faith, do not fear for I am amongst you. Your minds are more powerful than any weapon. Focus on the enemy and strike them dead with your thoughts!"

Strange advice. Was it a new Nyxifer weapon? Killing with the mind could be done, but Konrad doubted these acolytes had that kind of power. Or did Nyxifer boost their mental abilities?

Konrad erected a mental barrier around him and Sultan, just to be safe. As he aimed his weapon at Nyxifer, he realized the entity was too ethereal to be entirely present. He seemed to be phasing in and out, like a disrupted hologram. Not the right conditions to strike. If he missed, the red devil might hide and disappear for good.

The red-robed worshipers pushed back their hoods, revealing shaved heads, then they joined their hands in prayer and closed their eyes. They seemed to concentrate, as if linking their minds together. They also intoned a deep-throated vowel, and the strange vibration spread throughout the cave. Mind power?

A new contingent of android angels manifested in the cave. Good. They would be immune to any mind-killing vibes the acolytes might produce. Hovering above the crowd, the androids fired blue lightning on the enemy soldiers, who shot red beam weapons toward the vaults. The air sizzled with energy weapons fire, spreading the burnt smell of brimstone.

At the commotion of angel wings and weapons exchange between android and Cyborg, a few disciples opened their eyes and looked up. They abandoned their meditation to draw their red daggers. As more and more acolytes imitated them, the vibration created by their throaty chant weakened.

Nyxifer, looking upon the scene with disdain, did not intervene. Then the entity vanished. Konrad realized the red devil was never present in the cave, but speaking from a remote location. Where was he? Was he with Valka?

Then a flock of flying demons dove down from the high vaults and attacked the android angels. The flapping of wings unsettled the torches and spread the smoke with the smell of blood, as the high vaults came alive with the sizzling of blasters, the lightning of swords, and the screams of battle.

Konrad killed a few beasts, but he needed to find Valka and Nyxifer.

Blue lightning surged from angel swords to strike the demons, who screamed with distorted faces. Some disintegrated, some crumbled, others fell from great heights with a deadly thump, others still, twirled their disjointed wings in pure panic.

Konrad's invisibility cloak sparked and fizzled, leaving him and Sultan exposed. Drats! He forgot the special vibration around the altar and came too close. The same thing happened to Valka when she rescued him from that horrible stone.

Killer Krow spotted Konrad and threw a dagger at his head. Konrad ducked and the dagger clattered on the wall of the cave.

"Sultan, time to fight." Konrad unsheathed his sword. "Dive!"

Sultan banked and dropped, then dove upon Killer Krow's black hood.

Krow ducked and slipped on the floor slick with blood, lost his balance and fell. With a raging yell, he picked himself up and pulled off his hood, revealing his scarred face and skull. His dark eyes shone with hatred. "Come at me if you dare, General. Your insignificant angels cannot win against my demons!"

"Your demons? You do not command them." Konrad leapt off the tiger and landed carefully on the bloody muck. With his sword he hacked down the cuffs restraining the man to be sacrificed.

As the would be sacrifice rolled off the altar and crawled away in the bloody goop, Killer Krow stepped back, his hands looking for a weapon at his belt.

Konrad faced Krow blocking the altar stone, at the center of the wheel-shaped temple. "You are only a puppet serving forces you cannot control."

Krow pulled a blaster from his belt and aimed it at Konrad. "Since they want to destroy all angels, we have the same goal... in that regard, the demons serve me."

Konrad pointed his crystal sword at the blaster just as Krow pulled the trigger. Blue lightning surged from the angel weapon and neutralized the red blaster fire. "Sorry, but the weapons Nyxifer provided won't work against us... especially since we destroyed your master's main power source in his universe."

Krow stared at his blaster then threw it away and drew his sword. "The Exalted Master is stronger than you think. He draws power from many sources."

"Does he? Where is he? Where is Valka?" Konrad hoped she was still alive.

"Wouldn't you like to know?" Krow had a sinister smile. "Shame on you, General, being rescued by a woman and a filthy beast! But she will not save you this time. She cannot escape."

"Tell me where she is." So, Valka was alive. Konrad still hoped he could get to her in time. He stepped forward, pointing his blade at Krow's throat, grazing the skin.

Krow deflected the blade with his own and stepped back with a distorted smile on his scarred face. He snapped his fingers and a dozen demons dropped from above and attacked Konrad.

Deploying his wings, Konrad rose and struck the creatures with angel fire from his blade, ducking to avoid their burning acid drool.

Sultan flew to help Konrad, snapping at wings and planting his fangs in the furry black beasts, growling when acid from their blood and saliva burned his skin or his wings. Konrad slashed and stabbed demons with his sword in one hand. Then he drew his NK blaster with the other hand and started firing as well.

This almost seemed too easy. Were the creatures weakened by their master's lack of energy source? Good. The accidental detour through Nyxifer's universe had been useful after all. But Konrad wasn't any closer to finding Valka.

While Sultan fought the demons in midair, growling and biting and crushing skulls with his fangs, Konrad fired his blaster and sent blue strikes from his sword.

Two demons attacked him at the same time. He killed one with a blue strike. The other grabbed his left arm and bit him causing excruciating pain. Konrad dropped the blaster and severed the demon's head with his sword, but the pain in his arm got worse, dripping with acid, leaving a black burn on his white sleeve.

Then, seeing an opening, Konrad dove down upon Krow. The despicable man was trying to escape. But Krow had no special powers. Ignoring his lame arm, Konrad dropped on him, pinned him to the stone floor with his knee and pressed his sword to the man's throat. "Where is Valka?"

Even pinned to the filthy floor, Krow laughed, unafraid, unimpressed, not even fighting back. "You'll never find her. Her armor is ours now. Her power is ours."

Konrad wanted to smash the man's scarred face and drive his sword into his throat, but something told him not to. Killer Krow knew where Nyxifer kept Valka. Then, something even more disturbing surged in the man's demented stare. Something dark and fluid and oh so dangerous...

Krow emitted a curdling scream. Surging from the man's eyes, two rays of red energy struck Konrad's forehead, neutralizing his mental shields, and searing his brain like two hot pokers, sizzling as they burned his very soul.

Konrad lost his balance and collapsed under a pain he could not control. A loud cry escaped his lips unbidden. Pure agony, fiery hot and impossible to withstand coursed through his entire body. Mind-killing ability! Krow had it! And he was killing him.

Vaguely aware of his surrounding, Konrad saw Sultan's shadow attacking Krow and struggling against demons. Sultan's distraction allowed Konrad to somewhat recover, but what could he do against such powers?

As Sultan kept attacking Krow, Konrad managed to rise on his knees. He lunged at

Krow from below with his angel sword. The blue weapon penetrated Krow's flank, glowing blue and radiating light. Blood surged from the wound. Killer Krow screamed and collapsed, bleeding profusely.

Konrad pulled out his bloody sword then focused on killing the evil man's soul. He would never reveal Valka's location, and people like Krow did not deserve second chances, nor pity, nor mercy. Konrad concentrated his own mind-killing ability, asking the nearby android angels to strengthen his willpower.

Fortified by the will of the surrounding androids, Konrad rose and stepped up to Krow who still struggled to stand. Setting one heavy foot upon Krow's chest, Konrad grasped his crystal sword with his good hand and plunged it into the evil man's black heart.

So much hatred escaped Krow's dying stare. Konrad watched as the life drained from his enemy's face and body. But he felt no relief. Although the man had met his just punishment and Konrad had his revenge, the Nyxifer mission remained, and Valka needed saving.

Then, as if on cue, Nyxifer arose from the stone floor in a red whirlwind, holding Valka's armor like a shield in front of him. Was this a trap? Or was he bragging to antagonize Konrad? The evil master seemed more tangible than before.

Was he really here this time? Konrad wished he had his NK blaster, but he'd lost it when the demons wrenched it from him.

Then he had a crazy idea. "Sultan, grab the armor!"

The tiger leapt and bit into the armor, hanging onto it with fangs and claws as he flapped his wings. Nyxifer wavered in surprise but still held onto the armor.

Ignoring the demons fighting the androids overhead, Konrad sheathed his sword, spread his wings, leapt, and latched upon the precious artifact with his good hand in a locked fist. An armor with such powers must be strong and certainly wouldn't tear.

Then Konrad's mind whirled as he fell into a black vortex, tangled with Sultan, Nyxifer, and the armor, wondering where they might end up... and whether they would be alive or dead.

Chapter Eighteen

From the Command Deck of the *Blue Phantom*, Graziella the Merciful watched the monitors relating the progress of the battle raging in and around the Priory compound. It seemed the angels were gaining ground on the surface against the black-clad soldiers and the Cyborg, but inside the caverns, the demons never relented, and their numbers seemed to increase.

Her first officer, General Konrad Lagarde, had just killed Leader Krow in the sacrificial cave, but then he'd vanished with Nyxifer, the tiger, and the Valkyrie's armor. Now, they were nowhere to be found on scanners.

Graziella linked her mind to that of her First Officer. *"General, where are you? Are you all right? Where is Nyxifer? Is the armor secure?"*

No answer. How could he possibly be out of mind's reach? Had the red entity abducted the general through a portal to another universe? Not likely. Nyxifer wouldn't leave in the middle of a battle. He had too much to lose if this fight didn't go his way. He must be close, watching from a safe, hidden place... but where?

On the screen showing the sacrificial cave, the silvery androids fought the demons and flapped their metal wings, striating the space with blue lightning. Meanwhile, the biological angels in white uniforms liberated the last innocent prisoners from their cells, and those lying on many altars, about to be sacrificed. Graziella shuddered as she noticed women and children among them.

She made mind contact with an angel officer in the cave. "Transport the rescued prisoners to the safety of the angel fleet... along with the wounded angels and the deactivated androids."

Despite the two Azuran legions sent to the underground complex, the enemy numbers never diminished. No matter how many demons the angels slaughtered, more kept materializing out of thin air, and their numbers remained the same. This did not augur well for the outcome.

Nyxifer needed to be killed. That was the only way the angels could win this fight. Unfortunately, Graziella had no idea where to aim her upgraded NK weapons.

The monitors showing the surface of Taurus Secundus focused on the periphery of the smoking ruins of the Priory buildings. There, small angel crafts and flying androids exchanged weapons fire with armies of Cyborgs that surged from the base of the hill in rolling tanks and hovercraft.

Automated black harvesters hovered above the battlefield, lifting electronic body parts and biological matter to recycle. In the heat of battle? How odd! Then Graziella realized they were providing cover for the Priory soldiers pouring out of the caves.

"Target these harvesters," she ordered in her com system. "And clean the surface of Cyborgs and soldiers!"

"Captain!" A panicked angel voice burst and filled the room. "Demons are materializing inside the *Blue Phantom*! They spit acid and have sharp claws... and fangs. They are devouring the helpless non-warriors in their path."

Graziella called in her com. "Engineering! How are the shields holding?"

"They are holding fine, Captain." An android voice.

"Fine? Then why do we have demons onboard?"

"They must have the ability to rematerialize through our shields, Captain."

Graziella realized the foreign nature of the nasty creatures somehow allowed them to manifest through the angel shields. But this was not the *Blue Phantom's* first fight against a horde of demons.

Graziella must alert the other captains of the new threat. She focused her mind. *"Demons detected onboard angel ships. Follow my lead to sweep them off as I did before, deck by deck."*

She flipped the ship-wide communication switch. "Implement deck sweeps. Watch for acid damage. All angels on the ship, link your minds together to sweep each deck one at a time with a collective mental wave. Follow my lead. Remember your training.”

Then Graziella closed her eyes to focus on the task.

May the Formless One protect the angels... although, the Formless One never took sides.

* * *

Konrad cried out as his body slammed on a glassy floor, shaking him to the bones. He’d also suffered many acid burns and no longer held on to the armor. Where was it? Where was Nyxifer?

He could hear Sultan whimpering a few feet away, spread on the hard surface, in the green glow of a strange dome. And someone else was here.

“Valka!” Konrad rose to his feet on the glassy surface, glad for his non-slip boots, and ran to her, happy to see her alive.

“Konrad! Is it really you?” The happiness in her voice and the pure joy on her face warmed him, but she was half naked, barefoot, chained to the floor, and wore the same electronic handcuffs that had restrained Konrad’s powers when he was taken by the Priory.

“Let me help you.” Konrad knelt and examined the cuffs. He focused his mind on the mechanism and they popped open, freeing Valka. He held her close for a moment.

A growl of pain reached his ears. He kissed Valka's forehead. "Sultan needs help."

Valka crawled to Sultan. Couldn't she walk? "Konrad! Watch out!"

A swift shadow made Konrad duck as a searing red beam zipped past his ear.

The beam melted a small chunk off the green crystal dome and something sizzled, but the glassy material was thick and suffered no real damage. Too bad.

Then Nyxifer's infernal laugh filled the dome. The red entity hovered a meter off the floor, and the armor levitated beside him. The red hermaphrodite looked denser than before, almost solid... blood power.

As the hermaphrodite stared at Konrad, his black eyes gleamed with disturbing pleasure. "So, you thought you could kill me? You? A pitiful angel? You are no match for my powers."

"Is that why you left me my sword and didn't bind my wrists?" How Konrad wished he still had that damned NK blaster... He drew his sword and circled the entity, drawing the red devil away from Valka. He pointed his blade at Nyxifer and blue lightning surged from it toward the red devil.

A crimson shield rose around the red hermaphrodite, and the angel strike dissipated upon it. Nyxifer laughed. "I like to have my fun, too. I find you entertaining."

By the Formless One! But Konrad shouldn't swear. He called his brethren in his mind. *"I found Nyxifer. Focus on my position. I need backup."*

No response.

"They can't hear you." Nyxifer sneered and retaliated with a searing red beam as thin as a laser coming from his eyes. That was where Killer Krow had obtained this unusual ability.

Konrad caught the red beam on his crystal blade and it sizzled in the air. "What is this place? Where are we?"

Valka's voice rose behind him. "We are at the center of Taurus Secundus, floating inside the planet's molten core."

"And here you will die!" Nyxifer snapped his fingers and a dozen demons materialized inside the dome, spuing acid, growling, baring long white fangs, like giant murderous bats.

Deploying his wings, Konrad aimed with his sword and threw blue strikes of energy that sent them reeling, but a few of his strikes sizzled on the glassy dome, and each time, its light seemed to weaken. Could the Blue Crystal energy have an effect on the green material... or on the shield protecting it?

But more demons materialized faster than he could kill them.

With Valka and Sultan unable to fight, he was outnumbered. But not outsmarted. They still could win... if they survived. Now he struck not only the demons, but many parts of the dome with blue fire, noticing a weaker reaction from the shields each time. They were fading. The next strike, in the exact spot where Nyxifer's red beam had nicked the glass, created a long spark, then the light dimmed even more... as if the shields were so damaged as to be deactivated.

A glance at Nyxifer's scrunched face confirmed he must be right. Konrad struck the dome with a sustained burst of blue energy. The red devil pointed a finger at Konrad and more demons dove upon him and Valka.

Konrad saw Valka in a defensive stance. But without her armor, she stood no chance against the demons. He flew to her and Sultan, grabbed her waist and seized the tiger's paw.

Then Konrad closed his eyes to transport them back to the *Blue Phantom*, praying this wasn't a mistake, and the shields were damaged enough to let them through unscathed.

* * *

As she rematerialized with Konrad and Sultan under the glowing arches of the *Blue Phantom* Sickbay, Valka couldn't believe they were still alive. Konrad had saved them both... again. But three demons rematerialized with them, drooling acid and attacking with fangs and claws. "Watch out!"

To her delight, Konrad pierced the closest demon's heart with his sword. Two luminous android angels manifested above their heads and rained blue lightning on the two remaining demons, who screamed as their bodies twisted then disintegrated into dust.

Konrad sheathed his sword with a sigh of satisfaction and a spark in his deep blue eyes.

All around Sickbay, on perfectly aligned floating beds, wounded angels and civilians lay, with attending healers at their sides. The energy felt so good, Valka couldn't help but smile.

Two healers in white robes knelt beside the floating bed where the unconscious tiger lay. They applied their hands on the furry bunch of feline muscles.

One healer smiled at Valka. "His heartbeat is strong. He will recover. We'll see to it."

"Thank you for healing him." All the tension fled from Valka's body. Her legs collapsed under her.

Konrad grabbed her arm, helping her sit on a stool, next to Sultan's bed. "Are you okay?"

"I'm fine, just weak. Thanks." How humiliating to need help. But she felt lucky to be safe, among friends, in the harmonious aura of the Blue Crystal. Was this how mortals experienced life, constantly surrendering to weakness? "I feel like I can breathe again."

"Good." Konrad smiled at her with so much love in his deep blue eyes. "The healers will take care of you and Sultan. I have to report to the captain."

She noticed the black burns on his white sleeve. "Wait! What about your arm?"

Konrad shrugged. "It can wait."

Valka managed a smile. "Go. I'll join you as soon as I can."

He squeezed her hand, kissed her lightly on the forehead then vanished.

Valka sighed. Without her armor, she couldn't even dematerialize anymore.

As the two healers channeled blue energy through their hands and made it travel up and down the tiger's muscular body, Valka sat by the floating bed and caressed Sultan's head. Her hands no longer held the power to stop pain and delay death, but she could still comfort. "Don't worry, Sweetheart. You are in good hands. You will be back and leaping around in no time."

After a long life as a gifted immortal, nothing was worse than feeling powerless. But now, deprived of the powers of the Valkyries, Valka could feel the energy of the Blue Crystal pervading everything on the *Blue Phantom*. As her natural Zephyrian mind-reading abilities returned, she could again sense and read the collective minds of the angels on the ship. They were loving and peaceful, but still worried about Nyxifer, about the final battle to destroy him.

The tiger stirred, but his eyes remained closed. *"Sultan trust Valka. Sultan better."*

Valka rejoiced and kissed the big furry head. "I'm glad to hear you talk again, Sweetheart. The healers are taking good care of you. I shall return soon."

"Hold on!" One of the healers moved closer to Valka and applied both hands on the back of her neck. "You are still weak. This will help."

The hands felt warm and vibrant. For the first time in her life, Valka experienced the wonderful flow of angel energy. She felt comforted and her strength returned. "Wow. Thank you."

The healer nodded then returned to Sultan's side.

As she stood up, feeling much better, Valka realized she was almost naked. "Where can I find some clothes?"

One of the other healers pointed to a door in a corner of the room.

"Thanks." At her approach, the door lifted, revealing a closet lined with hanging clothes and shelves of neatly folded uniforms... all white.

Valka moved past the long robes. On the shelves, she selected and unfolded a shirt and pants and held them against her body. Too small. She tried the next size up, noticing the nearly invisible slits on the back for the wings. The garment fit her perfectly.

It felt strange to wear an angel uniform instead of a Valkyrie's armor, but the raw, uneven silk was surprisingly soft and comfortable against her skin.

On the bottom shelf she found white boots with the right fit. If only she had her weapons. She missed her dragon fang blade.

As if reading her mind, one of the healers raised her head. "The armory is the first hatch on the right in the corridor. It's always open. Help yourself to whatever you need."

"Thanks." Valka hesitated. "Did you just read my mind?"

"We angels read each-other's minds often, especially when we sense a brother or sister in need of help."

"Really!" Valka realized the Valkyrie's armor no longer shielded her thoughts from other mind-readers. She could no longer keep secrets. That would take some getting used to. "Let me know when Sultan is fully recovered."

"We will." The healer lowered her gaze, refocusing on her task.

Exiting Sickbay, Valka turned right in the corridor and recognized the hatch as it lifted to let her inside. she'd been in that armory before, on Azura, when Konrad showed her the new NK blasters. But she knew now she couldn't wield those. Since she wasn't an angel, she would have to stick to more conventional weapons.

She took in the many shelves and the weapons neatly aligned, touching them to feel the energy as she walked. She picked up a simple angel blaster, a blue sword, a crystal dagger, throwing stars, and a few short blades she could hide in her boots. She may not be able to conjure lightning through the blue sword like the angels did, but any blade could stab and slice, or be thrown from a distance and kill.

Feeling like a warrior again, Valka left the armory and followed the corridors with a new confidence in her step. She remembered the way to the Command Deck.

* * *

Konrad switched his weight from foot to foot to calm his nerves, as he stood on the Command Deck of the *Blue Phantom*, with officers and androids gathered, in front of Captain Graziella the Merciful.

The captain nodded. "So, although our scanners cannot detect him, we know where Nyxifer is hiding."

"Yes, Captain." Konrad must convince her to act quickly. It was the only way to win. "Inside a green crystal dome floating in the molten core of the planet. And I damaged the shields with Blue Crystal energy to get out. They are temporarily disabled."

"Our weapons cannot reach the core." The captain paced in a small circle, hands behind her back. "But you were able to lower the shields and dematerialize from there and rematerialize here."

"Yes, Captain. That's why I think a team can rematerialize inside the green dome as well... but we must hurry." Konrad held his breath when he saw Valka walking in, looking like the perfect angel in a pristine uniform. Only her peridot eyes betrayed her different nature... although they showed a hint of teal in all that green.

Captain Graziella acknowledged Valka and motioned for her to join the circle of officers. Then the captain faced Konrad. "I assume you have a plan."

"Yes, Captain. But we must act before they repair their shields." Konrad refocused on the problem at hand. "I propose taking a strike team inside the green dome with NK weapons. It's our best chance to kill the entity."

"I agree." But the captain seemed preoccupied.

"We should do it now." Konrad didn't want to miss this window. "I volunteer to lead the raid, since I've been there. I can visualize the place for the others to follow me inside."

Valka raised her hand. "I volunteer as well, Captain."

"Out of the question, Valka. You have no powers." The captain shook her head. "As for you, General, you can link your mind to the commandos to show them the way, but I will not risk the lives of biologic angels in this mission. A hundred androids are stronger and better equipped to succeed, especially if

Nyxifer uses his eye beams and summons a horde of demons.”

“Aye, aye, Captain.” Konrad was disappointed he wouldn’t get to kill Nyxifer himself, but he understood the captain’s logic. He was also glad Valka would not participate. Although a great fighter, without her armor, she would be vulnerable.

The captain closed her eyes to relay her orders to the android headquarters then she straightened. “They are getting ready. We’ll watch the monitors.” Then she turned to Valka. “Can Nyxifer use your armor against us? Did he unlock its power?”

Valka straightened and hesitated. “I didn’t give any clue on how to use the armor, but with this kind of evil... you never know what they might do. He could have gleaned the information from my mind.”

The captain nodded. “The fact that he didn’t use the armor against us so far indicates that he didn’t break its secrets.”

Valka released a breath she must have been holding. “That’s a relief.”

Konrad looked up as the bulkhead screens came alive with live feeds of the android headquarters. A hundred silvery units with a blue glow checked their weapons, thrusters, crystal drives, along with blue swords and NK blasters.

Valka stepped closer to him, almost touching, so close Konrad could feel her body heat. He could tell she was refraining from demonstrating affection in front of the captain. How sweet. But he must focus on the task.

As he linked his mind with the android commandos, Konrad detected no fear, no emotion, only logic and preparedness. This could work. He related the location of the green dome, drew a picture of the inside for them to visualize. He sensed their acknowledgement in his mind.

One monitor linked to the leader's synthetic eyes recorded the dematerialization as a blue flurry of sparks... slightly different from what Konrad experienced when he did it. Then the hundred androids vanished from the headquarters screen.

Konrad stared anxiously at the live link to their commanding officer. So did Valka, along with the captain, and the officers on deck. Then the monitor exploded in red and green flames, lots of static, and a horrible whooshing noise filled the Command Deck.

"What happened? Report!" The captain asked in a strong voice.

"Weapons exploding... Angel killing shields," another AI commando said calmly over the feed, before disintegrating in a flurry of static.

"Abort mission. Get out of there. Any survivors? Report!" The captain's voice shook.

No answer. Only blank screens and static. Too late.

Valka's eyes widened. "Did we just lose a hundred androids?"

Konrad sighed but it did not alleviate the guilt. "We acted too late. Nyxifer must have restored the shields to prevent intrusion after our escape."

"That was fast." Valka frowned. "What do we do now?"

Captain Graziella paced in a circle, hands behind her back. "To reach the core, we would have to drill the planet, but we have no tools strong enough to do that. Besides, it would take too long. Nyxifer would have time to escape."

"Maybe there is another way..." Valka's remark stopped everyone and silence filled the deck. "Any strong power source, like the Blue Crystal, can be used as a weapon."

Konrad read her mind and realized she was right. "If we can materialize and detonate a large enough chunk of crystal at the center of the planet, it will explode. It will also start a violent transformative chain reaction and destabilize the planet in the process."

Valka's excitement animated her teal eyes. "And if we can explode it inside the core, it will destroy everything... including the green dome and Nyxifer inside it."

The captain's eyebrows rose. "If done quickly, with the element of surprise, it could work. But Blue Crystal is very stable. To detonate it, we need a strong force of opposite and incompatible nature."

"You mean, like the red energy weapons Nyxifer provided from his own universe?" Konrad understood the concept. "We seized several of these from the Cyborg soldiers... including bombs."

The captain nodded. "Have all the red energy weapons transported to the *Blue Phantom* immediately."

"Wait!" an officer next to Konrad interjected. "How are we going to synchronize the transport of a crystal boulder with all that arsenal to the core, and rig it to explode?"

Captain Graziella the Merciful set her fists on her hips and took a deep breath. "We will have to transport the entire ship to the core and detonate it."

"Sacrifice the *Blue Phantom*?" Konrad realized the enormity of the statement, but losing one ship to save the entire universe seemed like an acceptable loss. Then he turned to Valka and noticed the sudden shock and sadness in her face. "What's the matter?"

She cleared her throat. "My Valkyrie's armor is inside the green dome."

"I am so sorry." Konrad took her hand. He understood what the armor meant to her. He could feel her grief and wanted to comfort her. "Maybe the armor will survive..."

"I doubt it. And even if it's not destroyed, it will be buried out of reach forever." A tear rolled down her cheek. "But it's the only way."

Konrad grieved for her, too. "Do not despair. The ways of the Formless One are unfathomable. There may be hope still, or even a joyous silver lining."

Ignoring the rules of conduct, Konrad took her in his arms to comfort her and caressed her flaxen braids as she snuggled against him.

Chapter Nineteen

On the Command deck of the *Blue Phantom*, Valka watched the monitors as angels worked frantically to prepare the ship for the attack on the planet core... Konrad among them. What a shame to sacrifice such a beautiful ship. She could only imagine what a loss it would represent for its captain and its crew.

Not unlike the loss of her armor. In all that feverish activity, fueled by angel hope, Valka couldn't shake the great void that washed over her. For thousands of cycles, she had followed the path of the Valkyrie as her only purpose. She did her duty. Her armor and the powers it gave her had become her identity, her only reason to live.

And now, facing its destruction, she realized she didn't know who she was without it. Yet, she would gladly sacrifice her Valkyrie powers to save the rest of the universe with all the angels who fought for what was right. It would probably save other universes as well. But mainly, Valka wanted to save Konrad. She wanted him to live.

In the midst of a war against pure evil, it was only a dream, of course, but she held on to that dream. Long ago they had found happiness for a short time. Maybe this time they could enjoy a lasting future together.

On the monitors, angels and androids secured loads of red energy weapons taken from the Cyborg soldiers, and fit them with explosive triggers. They also piled-up Nyxifer-killing weapons, to ensure the formidable blast found its intended target.

On the Sickbay screen, the healers dematerialized the wounded to other ships. Valka looked for Sultan but couldn't see him. She closed her eyes. *"Sultan, where are you? Are you okay?"*

"Sultan okay. Sultan on small ship." The tiger sounded much better.

"Good. I'll see you soon."

Other angels dematerialized the rescued prisoners, and the civilian angels dematerialized themselves off the *Blue Phantom*. Others yet, took the small fighters and yachts out of the landing bays and flew them, full of angels and rescued people, to rejoin the main fleet.

Captain Graziella manifested on the Command Deck. "Valka, what are you still doing here? You should be evacuating. Take the *Sweet Freedom* with General Lagarde and Sultan."

"Aye, aye, Captain." Valka hesitated. "You are going to rematerialize the ship remotely inside the molten core?"

"Remotely?" The captain cleared her throat. "That may not be reliable enough. We need a quick-thinking decision-making angel mind onboard."

"Then you are sending androids to guide the ship inside the core?" It made sense to Valka.

"Androids may not be enough. This could be our only chance to destroy that evil. We can't afford to miss. There is too much at stake."

Valka was confused. "What do you mean?"

"We need a sharp biological mind to make sure the explosion happens at the right moment, without warning, taking Nyxifer entirely by surprise. This is all or nothing."

Valka couldn't believe what she was hearing but didn't dare read the captain's thoughts. "You are sending an angel to die with the *Blue Phantom*?"

"I would never ask an angel to die." The sober expression on the captain's face said it all. "I'll go myself. I'm the captain. It's my ship and my responsibility. In ancient times, the captain always went down with the ship."

"Does Konrad know?" It seemed so extreme.

"All the angels know." The captain flashed a sad smile. "As you should know by now, we have no secrets."

"Are you sure it's the only way?" Valka felt guilty. Exploding the ship had been her idea. Graziella's ultimate sacrifice was greater than losing a magic armor... and Konrad told her the captain also had love in her life, something worth living for.

Konrad's voice filled the room through the com system. "Captain, preparations are complete. Only a few angels are still on the *Blue Phantom* and they will be gone in a minute. Should I give the order to our legions to evacuate the planet?"

"In a moment." Captain Graziella the Merciful straightened. "Evacuating too early might cue the enemy of our plan. Give orders to stand by, ready to dematerialize, but to keep fighting. We'll synchronize the evacuation with the attack within a fraction of a second. For this plan to work, we need total surprise."

"Aye, aye, Captain. Waiting for your order. May the Formless One assist you." The strain in his voice made it crack a little. Konrad definitely knew the plan.

"Thank you, General. Wait aboard the *Sweet Freedom* with your friends." She turned to face Valka. "Time for you to go."

Valka fought the tears in her eyes. All her life she had saved brave warriors, and now she faced one she could not save... not even if she had her armor. "Thank you, Captain, in the name of the entire universe. I hope you find eternal bliss with the Formless One."

"How angelic of you to invoke the Formless One, Valka. But you must know death is not the end, so rejoice. Things are the way they ought to be." The captain smiled. "Are you ready?"

Valka could not speak, her throat constricted by emotions unseemly for a warrior. She nodded instead. Being sensitive and vulnerable was not easy for her, but now without powers, she must get used to it.

The captain extended her hand and sent a strike of blue lightning in Valka's direction. Valka instantly found herself on the Control Deck of the *Sweet Freedom*, where Konrad was scratching Sultan's head.

"I'm glad to see you two have become friends." She patted the tiger's neck.

Her hand touched Konrad's and a pleasurable current coursed through her. He squeezed her fingers and smiled, and Sultan growled his approval.

* * *

Graziella the Merciful felt the collective sadness of the other angels, but she must ignore her feelings and focus on the mission. "Are all the angels off the ship?"

"No!" Leana, her mate, erupted on the Command Deck, ran up to her, and threw herself in Graziella's arms. "Let me go with you. We will be together forever."

Graziella steeled herself as she inhaled the sweet scent of her companion's hair. She felt the desperation in the tight hug. She understood Leana's distress and knew it was easier to die for a cause than to remain behind.

She caressed Leana's lush black hair. "We each have our destinies, Beloved. We shall meet again. Our souls are linked through space and time. We shall always find each other.”

“I don’t want to live if you die.” Leana choked on the words. As she looked up, her eyes shone with tears.

Graziella kissed her forehead softly. “And I want you to live. I’m doing this to save you, too.”

Leana wiped her tears. “I love you.”

“And I love you, too. Farewell, Beloved.” With a last kiss, steeling herself for the separation, Graziella dematerialized Leana and sent her to the fleet’s command ship.

Straightening her back, Graziella announced over the fleet-wide com. “All angels evacuate Taurus Secundus. On my mark... Three... Two... One!”

On one, Graziella dematerialized the Blue Phantom and rematerialized it inside the molten core of the planet. Silence surrounded her, and time seemed to stop as she swiped her console. She felt weightless. “Explosion in Three... Two... One...”

Graziella closed her eyes and took a slow breath. “May the Blue Crystal fire destroy all evil and purify this planet for the Formless One...”

* * *

Konrad winced as he watched, or rather felt the formidable detonation resonating inside his bones. Even from the control deck of the *Sweet Freedom*, at a safe distance in space, protected by angel shields, it was an awe-inspiring vibration. He closed his eyes to experience it fully.

In a mental flash, Konrad saw Nyxifer inside the green dome, clinging to the armor, his face distorted in agony, screaming as he realized he was dying and unable to stop it. Red energy leaked from his body, adding to the explosive power of the Blue Crystal.

When Nyxifer let go of the armor, his arms and legs were pulled away from his torso by extreme forces, and his head flew off in the air, as shards of green glass pierced his heart. Then green glass and body parts were blown to atoms in an explosion of light brighter than a sun.

As Konrad opened his eyes and checked the monitors, Taurus Secundus seemed to contract and expand, breathing fire and gushing molten lava from deep fissures. All the buildings and fortification walls around the compound were crushed to dust.

As he enhanced the images to see more details, the planet's crust opened and the rock split as the caves rose to the surface and gaped, spilling dying soldiers, human, Cyborg, and robotic automatons. Panicked demons screamed as they disintegrated into nothingness.

Eyes wide, Valka stared at the monitors. "Why are they vanishing?"

"Without the leader who summoned them, the demons return to dust." The only good thing about evil. "When you cut off the head, all the minions die."

As the view retreated farther back, Konrad could see new volcanoes erupting, spouting thick ash and rocks. Their fiery jets rose high enough into the atmosphere to reach the edge of space. The shifting crust folded on itself, forming new mountains, and the oceans migrated, flooding coastal military installations.

Then the planet tilted and reversed its poles. New wetlands appeared and old continents vanished. No living thing could survive such an upheaval. Besides, earthquakes would shake the planet for decades to come, and the air on the surface would remain toxic for centuries.

"Did it work?" So much hope in Valka's face. "Did we kill Nyxifer?"

Konrad was certain of what he saw in his mind, but he checked the scanners to be sure. "The detectors are showing no activity. No life whatsoever. No demons, no Cyborgs, no soldiers, no active technology, no Nyxifer, nothing."

"Could he have escaped?" Valka didn't sound quite convinced, as her voice carried worry and doubt.

Konrad felt it necessary to reassure her. "Not a chance. Besides, I saw him die."

"Are you sure you saw it?" She sounded hopeful.

"Angels do not lie." He smiled at her, so glad she was spared. "It all happened too fast for anyone to realize what was happening. The explosion inside the core destroyed the green dome. Also, the NK weapons onboard exploded as well, and those were rigged to target and destroy anything from Nyxifer's universe. Nyxifer died, but not instantly. He saw himself die. He realized he'd lost."

"Good. He deserved a villain's death." Valka stepped closer between him and Sultan. She laid a light hand on his shoulder. "I'm sorry about Graziella. She saved us all. She saved this universe."

Konrad cleared his throat. "Graziella the Merciful was a remarkable woman and an exceptional captain. She will be missed."

Valka petted Sultan then froze. "Is there any way to scan for my armor... in case it survived the destruction?"

Konrad realized how much she had sacrificed, too. He tuned the scanners for Asgardian tech. The results on the screens came up empty. "Sorry. No Asgardian technology detected either."

"Thanks. I appreciate your efforts." She offered a forced smile. "What happens now?"

"We'll place warning beacons around the planet and give it a few centuries to stabilize. In time, the crystal at its core will grow, and it will become an angel planet."

Konrad received a mental message from the Command Ship. *Mission completed. All units return to Azura immediately.*

Valka seemed to have heard the message in her head as well. "Let's go home."

Sultan shook his body like an excited kitten. *"Sultan like home."*

"Home..." Konrad never had a homeland... not in this life, anyway. He looked forward to returning to the angel planet, and making Azura his new home... with Valka.

* * *

A few days later, Valka in her white angel uniform, walked into the main Temple on Azura to attend the ceremony. The memorial for the angels killed in battle, and to honor the sacrifice of Graziella the Merciful, would be anything but sad.

A crowd of angels, all smiling in their white robes or in uniforms, filed into the circular temple and spoke in hushed voices. A dozen androids hummed as they floated around the large crystal boulder, high up, near the clear dome of the temple roof.

The soft harmonies emanating from the floating mass of Blue Crystal, the peaceful glow, the sweet fragrance of tropical flowers and incense, all contributed to the extraordinary experience. Here, Valka understood the meaning of serenity and happiness.

She also realized the depth of the crystal's influence on her. She could feel it vibrate through her entire body... as if she had no weight and might levitate at any moment, or leave her body and float near the ceiling. Definitely a new sensation, and she liked it.

She spotted Konrad near the altar at the center of the circular temple, so handsome in his white robes, speaking with other angels. She waved at him.

Konrad noticed her and waved back, then he walked through the crowd to meet her. "This way. We have assigned seats in the front row." His wide smile illuminated his blue gaze. "Are you okay? You look different this morning."

"Really? I'm fine... just a little light-headed." Could it be the joy of being with him?

He chuckled and offered his arm. "It's normal to feel strange the first time in this sacred enclave. The vibrations in the temple are exceptionally powerful."

"I can tell." Valka took his arm, enjoying his contact. She bathed in the strong energy pervading the holy place. "It reminds me of Asgard."

Valka noticed the lovely woman in white veils next to the Great Lady of Azura. "This must be Leana, Graziella's life mate."

"I believe it is Leana." Konrad indicated two seats.

They sat, facing the altar.

The angels hushed as the Great Lady stood up, blue veils fluttering around her as if she floated rather than walked to the center of the temple, until she stood at the altar, decorated with white flowers, directly underneath the large floating crystal.

"Today, we recognize the angels who fought bravely and died in battle, to protect this galaxy and this entire universe from the encroachment of pure evil. May they rest in the peace of the Formless One until called to duty again."

"Someone is requesting a voice." The Great Lady closed her eyes. "I am happy to announce that it is Graziella the Merciful herself. May her sacrifice be an example to all."

Then, high above the Great Lady, directly under the floating Blue Crystal, a giant ethereal cloud condensed into the precise shape of Graziella the Merciful, in white angel uniform, with her wings deployed.

Everyone in the temple stood up to show respect.

Angel Leana's face radiated light. She raised a hand to her heart.

Graziella the Merciful smiled. "All the angels lost in the battle join me to wish you well." Graziella looked happy and fulfilled. "My message to the Azuran angels is brief. My death was instantaneous and painless. I can confirm that Nyxifer and his demon hordes were destroyed. This universe is safe for now."

Valka exhaled a sigh of relief, along with all the angels present.

"The Blue Crystal is growing inside Taurus Secundus as we speak. In time, it will transform that planet into a blue glowing orb like Azura. All who land, or rather crash there will become new angels."

Then the spirit of Graziella the Merciful turned to Valka. "Valkyrie, I'm sorry to report that your armor was also destroyed in the blast. But your future looks bright and happy. You are now free to be whatever you choose."

"Thank you, Captain." Valka realized Graziella was right. Her armor may have been her source of power, but it was also a duty and a prison. No longer.

As Graziella the Merciful turned to her female companion, all the angels held their breath. "Leana, I will always love you. Don't be sad for me. We shall meet again and be happy together. Love is the strongest force in the universe."

"I love you, too, Graziella. I will always love you." Leana smiled through the tears.

Then, Graziella turned to the rest of the angels. "As for you all, I keep you in my heart and I wish you eternal bliss."

When Graziella blew a kiss to Leana and vanished, her lovely mate smiled through the tears.

Valka noticed again the musical harmonies and the sweet smells, as well as the special vibrations of the Azuran temple.

The Great Lady stepped forward and raised both hands to the crystal. "Thank you

O Formless One, for allowing us to commune with the loved ones we lost."

The Great Lady joined her hands together and bowed to the crystal, signaling the end of the event, then she walked – or rather floated – to the main aisle toward the exit, followed by the members of the Azuran Council.

Valka took Konrad's hand so they'd walk out together. "Do you think I have what it takes to become a true angel?"

He squeezed her hand and chuckled. "You already are, Valka. Your eyes are changing, and look at your feet."

Glancing down, Valka realized she was levitating a few centimeters off the ground. She willed herself down to the floor then walked with Konrad along the main aisle, then through the monumental doors, out in the sunshine.

From the shade of a blooming tree on the lawn, Sultan saluted them with a roar. Other large cats lounging with him in the grass joined in the salute.

Valka laughed at the spectacle and approached Sultan. She scratched his head. "I see you made new friends."

The tiger scoffed. "*Sultan like friend. Sultan like Azura.*"

"Glad to hear it." Valka turned to Konrad. "Did you hear that?"

"Yes." But Konrad stared at her face. "Your eyes! In this light, they look like Blue Crystal."

"Really?" Valka hadn't consulted a mirror in a while. "Cool."

Konrad squeezed her hand. "So, have you made a decision? Do you think you can get used to living here as an angel, with all the rules that entails?"

Valka remembered a time when she hated rules. "The rules are not so bad... and there are fringe benefits."

She faced Konrad and offered her lips for a kiss. The strength of his embrace and the passion in his kiss made Valka feel light again. Then a strong wind lifted her off the ground. Konrad rose with her.

As their lips separated, he smiled and his deep blue eyes shone brighter. "Look at you now!"

Valka realized the wind came from the flapping of her own wings. She had wings? They were hovering in midair, both sets of wings flapping.

As they landed slowly, Konrad smiled. "Did you know Azura is my favorite planet?"

"I know... and I like it, too... a lot. At the idea of living here, I don't miss Asgard so much." She read his mind and couldn't stop smiling. "It's not just the planet I enjoy, but the angels as well. They are like a family, a brotherhood. They care for each other."

"Yes, they do." Konrad pursed his lips. "Some more than others."

Valka exulted. "And what would we do here as angels? Can we live together?"

"Of course..." He had a devilish smile.

A delicious frisson course down Valka's back at the very notion. "And what would our duties be?"

"You could join me as I return to the Avenging Angels." Konrad pursed his lips. "Together, we could save the universe one mission at a time, using our powers and warrior skills to keep evil from overwhelming the galaxy."

"It doesn't sound so bad." Valka relaxed into his embrace. She had found a place to belong, with the man she loved, Sultan was having a good time chatting with other telepathic cats.

Konrad kissed her hair. "We can all be happy here."

She leaned her head on his shoulder. "Truth be told, I was getting tired of roaming the galaxy as a bounty hunter." She couldn't stop grinning. "I can see myself as an immortal warrior angel battling evil in the service of the Formless One."

The End

More books from Vijaya Schartz
Published by BWL Publishing Inc.

Blue Phantom series:
Book 1 - Angel Ship
Book 2 - Angel Guardian
Book 3 – Angel Revenge

Byzantium series:
Book 1 - Black Dragon
Book 2 – Akira's Choice
Book 3 – Malaika's Secret

Azura Chronicles series:
Book 1 - Angel Mine
Book 2 - Angel Fierce
Book 3 - Angel Brave

Chronicles of Kassouk series:
Prequel: Noah's Ark
Book One: White Tiger
Book Two: Red Leopard
Book Three: Black Jaguar
Book Four: Blue Lioness
Book Five: Snow Cheetah

Ancient Enemy series:
Book 1 - Anaz-Voohri
Book 2 - Relics
Book 3 - Kicking Bots

Single title sci-fi romance:
Alien Lockdown
Snatched

Archangel twin books:
Archangel Book 1 – Crusader
Archangel Book 2 – Checkmate

Also check out Vijaya Schartz's medieval
fantasy series
based on Celtic legends: CURSE OF THE
LOST ISLE

Book One – Princess of Bretagne
Book Two – Pagan Queen
Book Three – Seducing Sigefroi
Book Four – Lady of Luxembourg
Book Five – Chatelaine of Forez
Book Six – Beloved Crusader
Book Seven – Damsel of the Hawk
Book Eight – Angel of Lusignan

Vijaya Schartz also published
contemporary romance

Ashes for the Elephant God
Asleep in Scottsdale

Award-winning author Vijaya Schartz never conformed to anything and could never refuse a challenge. She likes action and exotic settings, in life and on the page. She traveled the world and claims she comes from the future. Her books collected many five-star reviews and literary awards. She makes you believe you lived these extraordinary adventures among her characters. So, go ahead, dare to experience the magic, and she will keep you entranced, turning the pages until the last line. Find more about Vijaya and her books at http://www.vijayaschartz.com